Bats, Rats, & Alley Cats

M. Barry Kirk

PublishAmerica
Baltimore

© 2005 by M. Barry Kirk.
All rights reserved. No part of this book may be reproduced, stored in a retrieval system or transmitted in any form or by any means without the prior written permission of the publishers, except by a reviewer who may quote brief passages in a review to be printed in a newspaper, magazine or journal.

First printing

ISBN: 1-4137-9372-X
PUBLISHED BY PUBLISHAMERICA, LLLP
www.publishamerica.com
Baltimore

Printed in the United States of America

Contents

Blood Rites 5
Fraidy Cat 11
Little Green Men 19
Christmas with the Phants 27
One Pink Unicorn, To Go 32
It's a Jungle Out There 41
The Bard's Goldfish 45
That Time of the Month 51
A Little Hair Transplant 58
Tough Guys 63
Rats in the Attic 72
Zombie Heart 79
The Alien with the Cookie-Crumb Face 85
Why Cats Lick Their Paws 91
Kai's Magic Marbles 97
It's the Little Things 108
The Living Trust Rubber Company 113
One Sure Cure for Writer's Block 121
The Lining behind the Cloud 127
A Taste of Fresh Salmon 135

For my children Ryan and Arielle, and for my wife Betty, who incidentally loves our backyard full of tropical fruit trees.

Blood Rites

Dr. Stanley Melnick stepped quietly into the busy Tri-City Hospital emergency room just as the wall clock struck midnight. Strolling past the prominent blood drive poster, he glanced around the ER entrance, and snorted in mild surprise.

There was no noise. No hacking coughs, no ragged screams, no shaking sobs, no creaking sounds of gurneys loaded with ill humanity being moved, no subtle idle background chatter.

There were no patients. At this hour, on a hot summer weekend, with a full moon out, there were no patients in the city's busiest ER. There should have been dozens of sneezing, moaning, abscessed people crammed into the waiting area, commiserating with select friends and relatives mustered up for the tragic occasion.

But tonight the ER was empty.

Stanley snorted once more, thoughtfully. Reshouldering his worn backpack, he resumed his slow stride and waved idly at the desk nurse as she looked up from her paperback novel.

"Hello, Dr. Melnick. So you're the senior resident working midnights this month?"

Stan Melnick snorted again at the obvious and continued his stroll into the emergency room. Behind him Nurse Quigley turned slightly and teased, "Why, I'm fine, thank you for asking. And stop snorting— it's SO unprofessional."

"Yeah, right." Stan grinned wickedly as he made a TRULY unprofessional noise and turned the corner into C booth, the central resuscitation room where the sickest patients were brought to be closely monitored and stabilized prior to hospital admission. Here any overdosed, stabbed, gunshot, and hemorrhaging victims would be brought to mark their personal space by their bloody secretions and their moans. C booth was the small central room in the big ER where the pulseless were resuscitated, where the diabetics in insulin shock were miraculously revived, and where the GI bleeders received their blood transfusions before being turfed to Medicine ICU. This was where all emergency medicine senior residents spent their on-duty hours, and where Stan loved to work the most. This was Action City.

Dr. Melnick ambled over to the day-shift resident physician he was relieving for the night. Stan tapped him on the shoulder.

Dr. Dean Erdman looked up from his virology magazine. A cute blonde in a lab coat smiled seductively out of a magazine ad at Stan.

"Hey, what's up?" Dean yawned his greeting as he stretched and bounced off his high stool. Two women in traditional nursing white, playing poker in the corner, glanced up briefly and smiled, nodding their heads in a silent hello. The rest of C booth was glaringly empty.

Stan chucked his bag under the counter as Dr. Erdman retrieved his briefcase, picking up his scratched white motorcycle helmet and faded leather jacket as he readied to leave. "There's gonna be some real heavy action tonight!" Dean joked.

"Yeah, and it's gonna be YOU if you don't sell that loud bicycle of yours," Stanley retorted.

Dean Erdman stepped close to Dr. Melnick and peered soulfully into his replacement's eyes. "Stan, I keep tellin' ya, you're not really livin' 'til ya live on The Edge."

Both doctors grinned as Dean made his way out of the emergency room. "Take care," Dean added. "I have a feelin' that somethin' real weird is out there, just waitin' ta happen."

The subsequent silence was briefly torn by the cough of an awakening motorcycle, followed by the lonely whine of its engine fading into the distant night. In the ER, playing cards were shuffled. Soft staccato noises from the overhead air vent murmured an obscure incantation and quieted reluctantly. Stan Melnick sat on his high stool staring at the closed cover of his staid Emergency Medicine periodical. Boy, he reflected to himself, this night was going to be slow.

If it had not been so eerily quiet, Stan would not have heard the stranger's feet shuffling hesitantly in through the open ER entrance. There was a muttering of voices, the crisp clear tapping of the triage nurse's shoes on waxed linoleum, and the sound of a curtain on one of the side booths being drawn aside. Shuffling footsteps followed the curtain. The creak of a chair and the rustle of the curtain's closure were swallowed by the ensuing silence.

Nurse Quigley poked her shiny scrubbed face into C booth and spoke to Dr. Melnick.

"Just a mild asthma. I'll get the junior—she's reading in the back library."

Stan glanced again at his magazine, sighed, and meandered out of the central room and over to the single closed curtain along the wall of empty, open side booths. The junior resident would have no trouble handling this case, Stan knew, but it didn't hurt to briefly check the patient himself. Besides, he was beginning to get bored.

"Hello I'm Doctor Melnick how are you tonight what seems to be the problem how is your breathing?" Stanley reflexively intoned as he surveyed the thin, mildly wheezing elderly man shifting nervously on the worn chair.

"Well, I'm…okay, Doc, it's…jus' my asthma is…kinda actin' up…this week."

"Well, let's see what we have here. Do you smoke do you have cats or dogs have you experienced any fever or yellow sputum when were you last in the hospital are you taking your meds have you ever needed steroids breath DEEPLY now." Stan swung his stethoscope from its usual home over his neck and applied it skillfully to this patient's scrawny chest.

"Uh," the stranger wheezed between intakes of air, "I…sorta ran outta…my asthma pills…last week," he finished lamely, casting his bloodshot eyes to the floor, clearly ashamed of his medical transgression.

Dr. Melnick straightened up, twirled his stethoscope expertly once and slipped it casually back onto the parking lot of his shoulders. Paternally crossing his arms in front of him, he gently scolded the old

7

man. "If you had come in for a prescription renewal when you ran out, you could have saved yourself some grief."

"Well...I was gonna...but I jus'...got this FEELIN'...real scary, ya know?...like somethin' terrible...was waitin'...outside...." A telephone suddenly shrilled, breaking the outside quiet, and making the elderly patient jump. Stanley felt a small, familiar knot of tension begin as he heard the nurse walking over to answer the phone.

Stan snorted as he stared past the patient, gently straining to overhear the faint one-sided conversation between the nurse and the phone. The sudden clatter of sharp running footsteps hit the air, and Nurse Quigley thrust her head past the frail curtain and into the cubicle.

"Man down, ETA two minutes," she stated in Medicalese. "Come on, the junior resident is on her way for this asthma. We've got bigger problems." She vanished, and her footsteps disappeared towards C booth.

"Sorry, gotta go! Don't worry, respiratory's coming, and your doctor will be here in a second. I'm sure you'll be just fine." Stanley felt the familiar anxiety grow as he mentally shifted gears to handle the new challenge about to enter the ER. He flashed his Reassuring Smile Number Two briefly at the perplexed old man and followed the nurse into the resuscitation room. The junior resident would momentarily arrive to handle the mild asthmatic; Dr. Melnick was now officially responsible for the new patient "found down," most likely unconscious, possibly even dying, who was about to enter his care.

Hands were gloved, IV lines set up, needles readied, and blood collection tubes prepared by the two nurses for the imminent Emergency. After a short wait the "man down" arrived on a gurney rushed into C booth by two puffing orderlies.

The man was old. Stan was certain he had treated more elderly patients in his nearly four years as a physician, but this patient had a, well, ANCIENT air about him, as though he were a desert-dried mummy just recently unearthed. His skin was pale white parchment with so many wrinkles that his features were severely obscured. Thin, shocking grey hair sprang stiffly from his scalp. A flickering of eyelids and a rapid, shallow respiration made this week-old corpse a lie told on itself.

"What happened?" Stan calmly asked the obvious but critical question of the nearest orderly.

"Someone outside said that the old dude was just standin' there, mindin' his own business, starin' at the front of the hospital," the orderly replied, "an' then he made this weird cry an' keeled over. That's all we know."

"Thanks." Dr. Melnick initiated his job as he had been trained, running through tests and procedures in a correct, logical sequence. The victim's airway was cleared, oxygen started, cardiac monitor attached, IV lines begun, clothing removed, and bloods drawn for the usual barrage of tests. The stranger wore no Medic-Alert ID, and in fact had no form of identification on his person. His dark, dirt-stained, pocket-less clothing revealed no clues to his predicament. The mystery man's quaint garments were dropped into plain paper bags at the foot of his bed, and a clean hospital gown was thrown over his chalky white body.

Stanley stared meditatively at the recumbent form of his patient. The stat blood sugar had measured within the normal range, and the hematocrit…"Is the 'crit spun yet?"

"I'm getting it now." Nurse Quigley scampered away to get the result.

Dr. Melnick mentally ticked off his initial resuscitation check list. The man's vital signs supported hemorrhagic shock, and with no obvious wound causing the blood loss Stanley was suspicious of a GI bleed. Despite IV fluids running full blast, tubes inserted appropriately, and resuscitation trousers in place and inflated, the man remained unresponsive and colorless, barely alive.

Quigley called urgently from the back room. "'Crit's thirteen! That's one-three!"

"Two…no, make that FOUR units o-negative blood STAT." Stan felt that warm glow of satisfaction of being on the right track of an important diagnosis. The picture now made sense. The man was probably one of the local alcoholics who had finally bled The Big One, although Stanley was positive he had never seen this particular patient before.

But upon completion of the full exam, Dr. Melnick snorted in puzzlement.

No physical evidence of a GI bleed, yet everything was pointing to acute blood loss. And the man's pupils were the strangest Stanley had ever seen, almost catlike. Also, something awkward about this patient's mouthful of teeth...Stan realized with a start that the arterial blood gas results should be ready by now, and hurried around the corner to the phone to call the lab.

One minute later he ambled back into C booth, studying his scribbling of the lab results. Glancing up, he stopped dead in his tracks.

The nurses were standing motionless, trance-like, in the corner of the room, staring hypnotically at the empty bed in its center. IV lines hung limply, blood bags were dry, and the patient was gone.

"What the..." Stanley was so surprised that he forgot to snort.

The sudden sharp creak of doors swinging open alerted the young doctor, and Stan brushed past the immobile nurses. Rounding the corner, he briefly glimpsed the back of a figure in a flimsy hospital gown as it disappeared behind the closing ambulance entry doors, into the shadow of the night.

Stan followed, crashing through the same swinging doors and out into the ambulance parking area, staring wildly about for his errant patient. The man's used gown was rudely deposited on the asphalt. Otherwise, the wide expanse of blacktop was empty. There was no naked pale elderly white male running towards the street, nor were there any witnesses who may have observed his sudden departure.

Stanley stood alone, huffing a bit after his brief exertion, staring right and left, but saw nothing. After convincing himself that his seemingly moribund patient had truly run off, Dr. Melnick stood pondering a few more moments, a solitary and discouraged figure in the still night air, then turned and slowly trudged back into the silent emergency room.

If he had just glanced upwards, into the night sky lit by the full moon, Stanley would undoubtedly have seen the silhouette of a well-fed bat flapping smugly away into the midnight darkness.

Fraidy Cat

Now I'm a rather big man and I don't scare too easy. I'm as strong as an ox, and most men, women, and vermin I can handle with no heat. But there are some things in life that just aren't natural, and probably would be better off if left alone. It takes a lot to admit that a man can run across something which scares him, and what I'm telling you now, don't go repeating, 'cause I'll probably deny it all later.

I'm a mover by trade. I've been working for Freight Line Moving Company for nearly seven years, and I'm pretty good at my job. I can move anything from office furniture to personal home stuff across the street or across the state. I take pride in my work, and won't scratch or ding your things even if it takes me an extra day to move them. I don't take any chances, but I've heard folk say that you can't be too careful these days. Now, I guess they're right.

Well, this one Friday morning, me and Roy are scheduled to move this one small family a short haul, and then do some office equipment transport downtown. Nice folks, a ma, a pa, one six-year-old girl, and not much stuff, really. They're moving into something real fancy nearer to the city, leaving an old pre-Revolutionary War country house. We get there bright and early that morning, and start loading the truck without much fuss.

Things are moving along just fine, with the truck just about full, and only a dozen or so boxes left to load, when the little girl comes up to me and starts talking.

"Hi. I'm Arielle. Do you like your job?" she says.

I keep handin' boxes up to Roy up on the truck. "Uh-huh."

So she stares at me for a while. "I have a job, too!" she offers.

"I like to go places. There're all kinds of neato places I visit with Fraidy."

I give her a quick glance and a short smile, but keep on lifting stuff into the back of the truck.

"Hey, mister, are you sweating?"

"Yeah, little girl, I'm working hard." I like kids, and some day I'll have a bunch, but you got to watch them careful so you don't trip over them or bump into them or some such thing.

"Sweat stinks," she says.

I grunt a bit as I shove a heavy box into the truck. "So does unemployment." But I give her another little smile so she doesn't feel offended or nothing, like we're friends. "Now be a good girl and go play with your dollies so you don't get hurt, okay?"

"But I want to play with Fraidy," she says. "That's my cat."

Oh, yea. We're supposed to put the cat into the pet carry box after loading all the stuff. I can do it now, though, and let Roy store the last few boxes.

"Okay, kid, go get your kitty. Kitty's gonna go on the trip with us, and we'll leave him with you at your new place." As you can see, I'm real patient with children.

"Fraidy's a *girl* cat."

"Really? Now that's special. Tell ya what, honey, you go and get *her*, and we'll put *her* in this pretty little box here, and help your Ma and Pa get you both over to that big fancy new house of yours."

"Fraidy's hiding."

"Where, hon?"

"In the house, of course." She looks up at me, like she's real put out.

Now trying to get the facts from some kids is sorta like pulling a rotten old tooth from a cranky jaw, but I got great patience, and I like kids, so I just give this small girly a smile and pick up the pet box. "Oh, good, then you can show me where she is, and help me put her in this nice warm box here, so we can get her to the new place, right? You don't wanna leave her here all alone now, do ya?"

The kid looks just a bit consternated, like she had a twinge of gas, but then she kinda brightens, and she says, "I can show you where she's hiding. Will that help you catch her?"

"Sure, kid, just show me the way." See, show a little patience, be nice, and people will usually just trip right over themselves to help. Even little kids.

So me and this six-year-old kid trek up the lawn and into the old house, after I holler to Roy to get the rest of the boxes, and I'll be back to the truck in a sec. With me carrying the kitty box and this urchin skipping along, leading the way, we get inside and go to the basement door and I switch on the hanging electric light bulb. I was down there earlier, and I know this is like the original basement to this place, looking like it was cut right out of the living bedrock under the house. It's a small, squared-off room, with just a few empty cardboards left on the cold stone floor. The single light bulb dangling from the ceiling makes sharp, irregular shadows on the floor, as we tramp down the creaky wooden stairs into this musty old basement, looking for the kitty.

I'm not 'specially fond of cats, being a dog man, but they can be useful, hunting down and killing rodents and such. Now rats are the real pests, and can carry all kinds of nasty diseases, as well as being able to chew up everything including electrical wiring. So I can tolerate cats pretty much, if they earn their keep. I don't fancy myself as much of a cat rustler, but this kid is scampering all around that basement, poking here and there, doing all the work, so I just kinda hang back, set down the kitty box, open its cage door, and wait for the little girl to produce kitty.

Well, she's looked just about everywhere and poked just about everything, and I'm about to say that kitty's not here, when she jumps up and snakes her hand into her pocket, and pulls out this little bell.

"Here, kitty, kitty," she calls out, shaking the bell. "Come here, Fraidy Cat, Arielle wants you."

I feel a yawn coming on and I fight it. I'm tired and I just wanna finish this job so we can haul the load, take a late lunch break, and hit the office job not too late. As I bend over to grab the kitty box so that I can take it back upstairs, I hear this weird popping noise, and a meow sound, and I look up to see this splotchy orange and black cat pacing back and forth, buzzing the little girl's shins.

By now I'm just a mite short on patience, being cooped up in this rock-walled basement far longer than called for, but I set down the kitty box again and start calling for the cat.

"Here, kitty. Come to your nice, warm box, kitty."

Fraidy stops buzzing the kid, turns her head, and starts staring me down, like she can't decide whether she should run or bite. The little girl stoops down to pick up the cat, but the animal hops away like a short-eared bunny, plunks down on her rump, and starts scratching at her neck. Then that fuzz ball self-righteously twists down and starts industriously licking at her privates.

"Hey, kid, can you pick her up and put her in this here box? We've gotta get over to your new house real soon, and you don't wanna leave the kitty behind, do ya?" I'm startin' to see the office job postponed 'til morning, if this keeps up.

The girl starts trying real hard now to catch the cat, but the dang fur ball just scoots away from her at the last second, real playful like, but wasting my time.

Well, all heroic adventures do have their moments, and I get my just reward with Fraidy crouching down and facing away from me. I make a quick grab for the furry feline.

Now as a kid, I once was handed some old shoebox by the boy across the street. He had thought it real entertaining to hide a lit cherry bomb in it, and grabbing that surprised cat gives me a quick flashback to when that firecracker in a shoebox blew up in my hands. There is a yowl, a loud pop, and that kitty is *gone*. I don't mean run away, either, I mean really disappeared into thin air. One second the cat is firmly clamped between my mitts, and the next, *bang!* I'm hanging on empty air.

So the girl puts her hands on her hips and starts talking. "Fraidy Cat!" she says. "That wasn't a nice thing to do to the poor moving man. Be a good kitty and come back to Arielle!"

I just kinda keep standing there, froze in one spot, waiting to see if any blood is flowing or if I have blown off a finger. I guess my jaw is hanging, 'cause this fluff of orange cat fur floats on over and gets stuck on my tongue. I close my mouth and choke on it, and then find myself in the embarrassing position of coughing up a hairball. At this point, girly skips on over and starts tugging at my pant leg.

"I know where she is! I do! If I show you, will you please promise to take Fraidy with us? *Please?*"

I can't see any blood, and all ten fingers are there and workable, so I turn to the kid and nod a bit. No telling what had gone blooey, but I haven't even been scratched, 'cept for my nerves.

Well, the little girl leads me over to the corner wall. We're farther away from the lone light bulb, with the shadows awfully dark, and I see nothing that could be a hole or a hiding place for a medium-size orange and black pussycat. Little girl points to the corner, where two rough stone walls meet the stained rock floor.

"She's in there. That's her secret hiding place."

I refrain from stooping over, but I look. There's no hole here, and no kitty, either. I fear the little darling's cracking up. I had no idea this could happen at such a tender young age. I kinda look down on this little girl, and start to develop a real pitiful feeling deep in my gut.

Then the kid seems to get another of one of them ideas. Fishing around in her pocket, she pulls out a one-inch long stub of hotdog. Sometimes I wonder how children can manage to walk around with all the crud they stuff in their pants.

The girl looks up at me with this real practical look on her face. "Fraidy just loves hotdogs. I'll bet she'll come out if you feed this to her." And she hands me that piece of old, smelly hotdog.

About now I get a premonition of things to come and I stifle the sudden urge to call it quits, forever, and retire before I'm forty. I'm feeling mighty flustered. I can already feel some of them grey hairs starting to sprout. But backing down from a challenge from some six-year-old girl is more than I can bear.

I cough out another piece of orange fur before I speak. Real quiet-like, I say, "Sure, kid, no problem." Then, feeling like the solitary marine ordered to recapture Hill 29 from the enemy, I get down on my hands and knees and look real careful at that corner. Nope, no hole, no nothing. I reach out and touch bare wall and floor. Solid as rock, which it is, anyhow. Looking real close at the corner, I notice that it's still cold, hard stone. Then I begin wondering about just who will be first to register in the psychotherapy ward, me or the kid.

"No, no, no! You have to squeeze your eyes shut real tight, and think like you're the wind, and let your arm just blow through the hole." Then, under her breath, "Goodness! Can't grown-ups do anything right?"

Great. The kid is turning loony tunes. But I've got this stubborn streak in me, and I can never give up 'til I'm licked, and I'm certainly not licked yet. So I do like the girl tells me to, screw my eyes shut tight and pretend like my arm is hanging out the car window, with the wind blowing around it. Gripping that piece of stinky hotdog, I concentrate real hard and almost feel like there is a breeze on my arm. Creeping forward, I shove my arm way out in front of me and suddenly feel like I've pushed it through a hole. Feeling around, still pinching that wiener, my fingers brush against some dirt and maybe some grass.

I'm just contemplating what grass is doing twelve feet or so down underground, just beyond a wall of rock in somebody's old basement, when I feel a little sniff and a wet nibble on the hotdog. Dropping the kitty snack and blindly grabbing, pushing aside the grassy stuff, I shove against a big warm furry thing. I then manage to clamp my digits on this thick, muscular animal leg, which seems kinda stocky for a little alley cat. As my hand grabs onto the limb and maybe some grass, I hear a deep funny growl, and suddenly a horrible burning pain tears down my arm.

Well, I tell you, I jump back so fast my sweat gets left in midair. I mumble something naughty which I belatedly pray the little girl can't understand as I charge up the stairs and outta the house into the late afternoon light to take a close look at my hurting arm. Sure enough, there are three horrendously deep scratches from my elbow to my wrist, dripping with my own blood.

It just so happens that across the yard is the little girl's folks, stuffing some odds and ends into a minivan. I quick-march up to the dad, and start talking.

"Excuse me, sir, but has your cat had all its shots?" I try to force the shakiness from my voice.

"Eh? What shots? Our cat?"

"Yeah, sir, you know, that Fraidy cat of your daughter's. She's got no funny feline diseases, does she?" My voice squeaks for the first time since early puberty. "I mean, just look what that dang-nabbed cat did to my arm here!"

"Well, yes, hmmm…Nasty scratches, mister. No, our cat's not sick, but Fraidy never could have done that to you."

This whole family is turning out to be real dense, and now I can begin to see why the kid has turned out so affected. "Well, why not?" I demand.

The dad just stands there, looking at my bleeding arm, and shrugs. "We have always kept Fraidy inside the house. Never let her out."

"So what?" I feel a warm flush angering my face.

"Had her fully declawed years ago."

I look down at the blood trickling onto my hand, and notice that my fingers are still clamped on a gob of grass I musta pulled out down in that basement while grabbing at that animal. The grass is colored bright red, and a little chunk of light blue-colored dirt is sticking to the square, black roots. And as I'm staring down at it, a set of three tiny eyeballs on tendrils poke out of that blade of grass and gaze accusingly back up at me, just before my fingers start shaking and I drop the unworldly thing.

I stand there in deep, thoughtful reflection for a few special moments, feeling what's left of my blood drain outta my head. I start thinking over what had just happened, and wonder exactly where my arm had been. I try to picture just what manner of critter from what alternative universe had torn me up. And I wonder whether them rabies vaccines are routinely given to the pets in the farther outskirts of the galaxy.

Without another word I turn and walk up to the truck, where Roy is waiting. He looks down at my arm, up at my face, and climbs into the passenger seat. That Roy, he sure knows how to size up a situation, without wasting a lotta time jawing about it.

"We're leavin'," I state as I climb into my driver's seat, slam the door, kick on the engine, and pull away from that old house. I don't even look back in the rear view mirror.

Little Green Men

The black saucer-shaped spacecraft eased down onto the empty field in a most self-confident manner, and from its bowels three little green men rolled out to plunk onto the dewy grass. They promptly crawled, noiselessly and unobserved, to take cover behind an adjacent low bank of shrubbery. The dark flying saucer slid complacently back into the inky moonless night, leaving the heavily armed and eminently trained alien invasion force isolated and concealed.

The black air remained chill and silent. In the near distance, a muffled automotive engine crescendoed and then dopplered away. Captain Ahdoo of the Imperial Invasion Force turned resolutely to his most junior sublieutenant, Snuf, and gave his first General Invasion Order: "I want my diaper changed, NOW."

Snuf scurried on hands and knees to his Captain's side, careful not to catch his uniform diapers on the underbrush. As he bent to his task, Very Sublieutenant Snuf hissed the thought that had been on his mind since landing on this backwoods planet just moments before.

"I had understood that the atmospheric temperature of this locale was classified as SUBTROPICAL. This is not as reported. I feel COLD." There was a glimmer of a tear in one eye, as he finished his diapering task and turned to glare at his immediate superior, Sublieutenant Gah.

Gah scowled resolutely back at the more junior officer. He retorted with only a trace of drool revealing his own discomfort. "As planetary rotation allows higher enthalpy levels, ambient temperatures will ascend into the high blinkeys, as I predicted earlier. So shut up and act like a soldier."

Snuf cringed under the browbeating. "Aaaaw!" he cried, softly. Captain Ahdoo and Sublieutenant Gah eyed each other thoughtfully, and then together slapped Snuf into a tearful silence. True, they were clothed only in field diapers, and the night's coolness was distinctly unpleasant on exposed green torsos and extremities. However, an Imperial Invasion Force soldier must always remain strong and fearless, no matter how chilly he felt. The Captain plumped his well-padded posterior down and took out his invasion plan viewer, stoically ignoring the unpleasant climate.

Meanwhile, Sublieutenant Gah found opportunity to throw a superior glare down on Snuf. Gah edged closer to Snuf and muttered angrily, "Get a grip, sublieutenant. It's just one eighth planetary rotation until increased solar radiance will make this area toasty warm. Our spy recorders are never that far off from the actual conditions." Gah sniffed at Snuf's diaper. "You have wet your uniform. Change it."

Snuf nodded in submission, calming himself in a soldierly manner. Captain Ahdoo had by now completed his study of the micro-condensed invasion plans, and stuffed them back into his fresh diapers. Noting Very Sublieutenant Snuf's attempts to change himself single-handed, he growled, "You should have thought of that BEFORE we landed to take over this planet. I doubt that you'll be finding any servo-uniform changers on THIS dump."

Very Sublieutenant Snuf choked back more tears. Now he was cold, wet, AND humiliated.

The Captain softened. He did not want such an important mission starting with discord among his men, with possible ensuing tantrums. He crawled over to his more junior sublieutenant, plunked his thickly padded (and dry) rear down, and congenially swatted Snuf on the shoulder.

"With this mission under your diapers," he said, "you'll be able to pick a retirement planet, a large home with servants, and several fat mates." Then he pointed afar with one pudgy green hand. "Let's creep over to that attractive structure just beyond the large box of sand," he burbled. "We'll be able to better review our plans and available resources from that sheltered position." And he proceeded to crawl confidently over to the location indicated, as an intergalactic commando leader should, followed closely by the other two invasion force members.

Not so very much later, as the leisurely rays of the dutifully rising sun dribbled its warm glow onto the three slumbering green men, an unexpected noise startled Sublieutenant Gah into raw wakefulness.

"Now what have we here?" Mr. Pruit, the elderly custodian, boomed in his deep voice as he found himself interrupted in his morning sweep of the nursery school play yard. He had stumbled upon the interplanetary invaders quite by accident, and now stared down at the three little green aliens with a mild expression of shock on his aged, angular face.

Very Sublieutenant Snuf jolted awake, assisted by an elbow from a distressed Sublieutenant Gah, while their Captain continued to snore. Gah slapped Snuf's face.

"You dope! You were supposed to be on guard duty!" Gah whispered to Snuf.

"But…but…but…"

"Oh, shut up. The damage is done. We are discovered. I would subjugate this monster, but his large size confuses me. I thought the aliens on this planet were significantly smaller."

"Uh…that's what the field report said. Should we awaken the Captain?" Very Sublieutenant Snuf was also staring up at the immense form of the custodian. He chose to follow his senior sublieutenant's example, and cowered in fear.

Mr. Pruit scratched his liver-spotted head, and then gathered up the three green non-resisting forms and carried them over to the preschool office. Mrs. Garfield, in charge of childcare and that kind of stuff, had arrived early as usual, leaving her office door open. Mr. Pruit entered the office and gently placed the three tiny aliens into the office crib. The two awakened invaders defiantly stuck their thumbs into their mouths. They were a superior race, and could not be made to talk. Captain Ahdoo continued to snore.

Mrs. Garfield was equally shocked when she saw the aliens, and after a moment of self-composure, she turned to Mr. Pruit. Her voice was stern when she finally found it. "Who painted these poor little babies GREEN?"

"I don't rightly know, ma'am. I found 'em in the play area, dressed only in their little dye-dies. Somebody musta dropped 'em off early or somethin', and then somehow they got inta some green paint. Curious." Mr. Pruit scratched his head speculatively. "Ya know," he continued, "I don't rightly recall havin' any green paint ta speak of. And the tool shed was locked solid."

Mrs. Garfield sighed. "Well, we'll just have to scrub them clean, and make some calls. This is highly irregular." She inspected the invaders more closely. "And it looks like they all need changing, too."

Just then, young Miss Lee, one of the preschool teacher aides, entered the office. Sublieutenants Gah and Snuf swivelled their eyes in her direction. While thumbs remained tightly clamped in clenched, toothless jaws, small lines of drool snuck out of the corners. Miss Lee was quite shapely, indeed.

Miss Lee spoke, angelically. "Oh! What has happened to these poor sweet babies?"

"Don't rightly know. Just found 'em near the sand box, painted green. I just don't know. Well, I got work ta do. See ya." Mr. Pruit was clearly agitated, and quickly left the office.

Officer Snuf let out a small sigh of relief. He preferred the shorter, rounder forms of the women. Especially that of Miss Lee.

At this point Captain Ahdoo came awake.

"Uh...where...JUST WHAT THE HELL IS GOING ON HERE?"

His sublieutenants cogitated on the proper response to their Captain's wrath. They elected to whimper.

"Oh, goodness! They're all crying! I'll bet all that thick green paint must be very, very uncomfortable." Miss Lee had a strong mothering instinct. She picked up the two whimpering sublieutenants, while Mrs. Garfield handled the larger mass of the incoherently screaming and writhing Captain.

"I know what!" Miss Lee continued. "Let's all take a bath!"

Sublieutenants Gah and Snuf abruptly stopped sniveling. A nude romp with this cute round woman-thing sparked their less-than-puritan instincts.

The Captain, carried by Mrs. Garfield, had calmed himself down somewhat, with the inadvertent aid of a pacifier shoved into his superior toothless mouth by his abductor. He signaled to his officers with his toes, and commenced to relay messages via Advanced Vartian Toe Talk. An interstellar commando was not a being to mess with.

Sublieutenants Gah and Snuf, being trained military officers, reluctantly stopped wriggling up against Miss Lee's svelte body, and commenced a careful study of their Captain's toes.

"PLAN ONE PLANETARY SUBJUGATION A MISERABLE FAILURE STOP ALTERNATE PLAN TWO IS NOW IN EFFECT STOP PLAN TWO GOAL IS OBLITERATION OF THIS CAH CAH DOO DOO PLANET UTILIZING BARTHROW THERMO-STELLAR IMPLOSION DESTRUCTOR STORED IN MY SHORTS STOP UPON INITIATION OF TORTURE OR PREFERABLY EARLIER A VOLUNTEER MUST SNEAK AWAY AND INSERT BARTHROW DESTRUCTOR INTO COMPATIBLE LOCAL ENERGY SOURCE STOP THIS MEANS YOU SNUF STOP STOP THAT SNIVELING STOP SNUF WILL INSERT BARTHROW AND SET TIMER FOR THREE MORTUMS STOP I WILL SIGNAL STARSHIP FOR IMMEDIATE DEPARTURE STOP WE WILL LEAVE THIS POOP HEAP OF A PLANET IN A BLAZE OF IMPLODING GLORY STOP OUR NAMES WILL BE EMBLAZONED ON DIAPERS THROUGHOUT THE KNOWN UNIVERSE STOP WE WILL AARGH OOOGLE SNORF"

Mrs. Garfield had noticed the dancing toes, and could not resist a tickle as she placed the chunky Captain on a changing counter. "Ooh, you are SOOO cute! I just want to take you home and EAT YOU!"

"AHH! CANNIBALS! WE MUST ESCAPE AT EARLIEST OPPORTUNITY!!" Captain Ahdoo was writhing on the counter, straining militantly not to giggle with the tickly feet torture.

Very Sublieutenant Snuf was carefully placed on the floor as his superior sublieutenant was readied for the next diaper change. Gah called down to him in apprehension.

"The Captain is being tortured! We must carry out his last wishes. We can only pray to Urtach for his survival."

Snuf was ready for action. "Look! The woman-thing is removing the Captain's uniform. We must recapture the Barthrow Thermo-Stellar Destructor and carry out this planet's destruction!" Snuf wiped a piece of drool from his chin, and sighed quietly. "Unfortunate. I thought that I had a chance with the cuddly one."

Sublieutenant Gah blinked at Snuf in understanding. He, too, had briefly entertained decidedly lecherous thoughts regarding these lowly but somehow wholesome giant creatures.

While Snuf remained on the floor, awaiting opportunity, Sublieutenant Gah was given Miss Lee's full attention on the changing table. Just then, Very Sublieutenant Snuf had his chance handed to him on a silver platter.

The Captain's soiled uniform diapers were tossed down by Miss Lee into a diaper pail, which incidentally did have a silver platter-like cover. Dropped from the opened diapers, sealed in its molecular plastic bag, a small flat black object with a bright red warning label was now lying on the floor, not two fidgets from Snuf. He secretively crawled over, deactivated the sealant with his gums, and pulled the object free of its moisture-proof bag. It was the Barthrow Thermo-Stellar Implosion Destructor.

Snuf's Polyfrequency Energy Examination apparatus, efficiently disguised as his diaper pin, guided him to the nearest unsheathed energy coupling. A trained trooper, Snuf scrutinized the Barthrow, quickly dialed the timer setting, activated the thermo-stellar controls, and tongued off the safety. The Barthrow device began ticking ominously. Snuf trembled with anticipation as he prepared to insert the double metal prongs of the destructor into the indicated wall plug, which was foolishly obstructed by some simple safely mechanism. Snuf had never undertaken such an important assignment before. This could mean a promotion to full Sublieutenant. Then Sublieutenant Gah could no longer slap him in the face with impunity. Snuf chortled as he began to pry the hopelessly inadequate plastic child-proofing device off the electric receptacle.

"You sneaky little devil! You just couldn't wait to creep away and hurt yourself!" Miss Lee whisked Very Sublieutenant Snuf away from the wall socket, inadvertently knocking the Barthrow Device away from his pudgy fingers and out the open window.

Very Sublieutenant Snuf let out an anguished wail. Having observed the inept proceedings from the changing table, Captain Ahdoo and Sublieutenant Gah harmonized their grief with their subordinate.

"Oh, now they're all crying. We'll just have to put them in the sandbox until their bath is ready." The two ladies carried the squalling infants out to the play area. As they turned and walked away, Mrs. Garfield turned to Miss Lee. "Good grief! I've never seen such cranky little brats! Let's hope we can clean off that horrid green stuff and return them to their mothers before lunch!" The ladies disappeared around the corner of the office.

"Silence!" Back in the sandbox, Captain Ahdoo slapped his sublieutenants until he had their full blubbering attention. "Our plans for world conquest have been crushed. Our attempt to vaporize this waste pit has been foiled. I say let us escape this miserable wee wee hole now and call it a draw. I, for one, do NOT intend to be tortured again."

Sublieutenants Gah and Snuf blinked back their oozing tears. They were failures, and probably would spend the next twenty decidongs tending soilant mines, but the prospect of being held captive here, with impending torture, appealed even less. Maybe they could come up with a good explanatory fib later. For now, escape was the first level priority.

Captain Ahdoo grunted and passed wind. A smile briefly lit his chubby face. "There. I have signaled the starship. It shall descend momentarily, suck us up, and we will hastily depart this mucoid drool of a planet." The Captain's eyes were stern. "Just keep your babbling mouths SHUT until I can come up with a reasonable excuse for YOUR blundering."

Sublieutenants Gah and Snuf nodded hopefully. Just then, a shiny black disk-like spacecraft dropped down to just above their bald green heads. Hovering low in the air, a long thick nozzle lowered down to the waiting troopers. The unsuccessful invaders were suctioned up, and then the dark spacecraft lifted silently up to vanish into the bright morning sky. Moist depressions in the sand testified that only moments before three small bellicose posteriors had rested there.

Old Mr. Pruit sauntered out from behind the tool shed, scratching his head. He thought he had glimpsed something hovering over the sandbox, out of the corner of his eye, but nothing seemed to be there now.

As he turned back, Mr. Pruit noticed a small black box-like thing on the ground by his foot. It was lying there in the dirt by an open window, as though someone had just tossed it out. He picked it up and examined the strange thing closely. There were some bright red Japanese-looking markings on one flat black surface, and two short metal prongs projecting from the back. The device seemed to be emitting a ticking sound. Being the curious sort, Mr. Pruit ambled over to a nearby wall receptacle to plug the thing in and see what it could do.

Christmas with the Phants

It was the fourth scorching summer after the third global nuclear meltdown, when Arnold Zigalot first noticed the phants. He was crouching at the kitchen sink, licking crumbs off the dinner dishes, when he glimpsed a fist-sized, red, shiny head with two antennae and a pair of cross-chomping mandibles peering around the corner. Arnold froze—phants always made him nervous, especially after the Farinachi boy tragedy—and the chitinous, red, glistening body of the lead phant scurried around the corner on her six spindly legs. Following blindly behind, a long line of identical puppy-sized insects advanced into the kitchen.

"Now, just what do ya think you're up to?" Arnold spat. He really did not like phants. Nobody did.

"We are passing through your domicile in search of nourishment. Have you anything to eat?" the lead phant warbled hopefully. She seemed fatter than the rest. Probably the head worker phant.

"This is not a domi- dumi- dum- This is my 'HOUSE,'" Arnold corrected with a hiss. He would not tolerate academic belligerence.

"Yes. Correction. Your homicile."

Arnold gritted his teeth. One molar crumbled. Arnold despised phants. They were arrogant, and greasy, and disgusting to look at. What pests.

The lead phant took a quivering step towards the ice box. Arnold stepped between that threatened appliance and the phant. It looked like another showdown, Arnold thought uneasily. The first days of every hot spell were like this, with phants invading his homissile- homiss- whatever. But lately, the phants were becoming more aggressive. And they seemed just a tad bigger this year, too.

"We are hungry," the first phant whined. "We want food. Now." She stepped forward with one foot, tentatively. The quivering line following behind her mimicked the move.

Maybe confrontation was out this year, Arnold decided, as a dribble of sweat traced a path down the faint yellow stripe on his back. His single remaining bloodshot eye squinted in a supreme effort of concentration. Scratching the stubble of beard sprouting from his left ear, an idea reluctantly slithered into his awareness.

"But if you eat anything now," Arnold pleaded, "you won't have any appetite left for your Christmas present."

Fat phant touched one hairy foot to her mid-torso. She seemed to be consulting something for a moment. Then she spoke.

"Christmas is your human party during the cold time. Now is the hot time. We are hungry now."

"Oh, yeah," said Arnold. He was so forgetful these days. "That's right. It's not Christmas, not yet." He thought for a moment. A radioactive decay sequence triggered a long unused neuron in Arnold's brain, and he had a rare inspiration.

"But tonight is, uh, Summer Solstice Night. Couldn't you all just wait a few more teensy hours for your present? It's a tradition, ya know." He would be sweating profusely now, if he knew how to spell it. Phants made him nervous.

There was another insufferable silence as Numero Uno bug paused to digest this new information. Finally, she spoke.

"Understood. If you have a gift for us we will wait. We will commune now with the Queen Mother and return after the golden orb retires with its light." The big insect paused as Arnold registered a blank stare, then it added a few choice words. "When it's dark, you mammalian moron."

The lead phant abruptly swung about and led her line of sisters out of the kitchen, through the living room, and out through a large old crack in a corner wall. In true phant fashion, the line of red bugs circled into and back out of Arnold's kitchen, obediently following the faint trail of greasy yellow pheromones deposited by their leader.

Arnold almost thought he caught faint wisps of conversation, sounding like, "Say, this is fun," and "Presents! I love presents!"—but he could not be sure. He held his breath until the last ugly red torso vanished from view.

"Who were you talking to, dear?" Mrs. Zigalot, awakening on the sofa in front of the glowing TV, quavered. She slept so much these days. And she had become even more retiring since her facial warts had begun to glow that brighter shade of green. Arnold, as always, pretended not to notice his spouse's gradual deterioration over the years. One had to be very forgiving in these post-nuclear-holocaust times.

"Phants again," Arnold intoned. "I've got to come up with something by tonight to get rid of them," he continued, "or they'll be here 'til Christmas."

"Did you say Christmas? I thought it was summer again." Mrs. Zigalot had pulled her gaunt teenage frame up, and now limped slowly toward Arnold on her knobby, hairy feet. The flickering shadows from the TV tube revealed brief glimpses of her stooped young form. "My bones ache," she murmured.

Arnold smiled. He vaguely remembered that he loved tender moments such as these. His grin widened. But a small crack started in his right upper lip, so he quickly ceased the effort. Then he grudgingly recalled his current dilemma.

"What should I do, love?" he bleated.

"I just don't know, Arnie, honey," his wife sighed. "Those phants are too big to squish this year. Why not poison 'em while we're out tonight? We still have the phant bait we bought last Christmas."

"Christmas? Is that coming up again?" Arnold muttered. But the phant bait was a great idea. He wasn't sure why he had not thought of that solution himself. Must be too tired.

"Where's the phant bait, my love?"

"Under the sink, in front of you, dear."

Arnold looked down. Wow. There it was. At least three brick-sized packages, maybe twelve, wrapped in plain brown wax paper, with the word "YUMMY" printed in large red block letters on each wrapper for the phants' benefit. Stamped in small blue type below, in a shade guaranteed invisible to phant vision, was the warning, "Poison—for suicide or phant control only."

"I know what. I'll put these out tonight, in front of the refrigerator, and tie a nice bow around the top. The phants will think it's their present." Then they will eat it and die, he concluded silently. The thought gave him a warm, almost nuclear glow, deep inside.

A new inquiry smoldered into his radioactive awareness, and he spoke.

"You said we are going out tonight, love chunks."

"Yes, hun. My dearest friend, Belinda, or Melinda, or something, said that she had heard her friend talking about some big lawn party tonight. She said she's gonna crash it. I wanna go too, sugar lips."

"Oh, I do love parties," Arnold said as he carefully stacked each brick of phant poison with the "YUMMY" word facing out. He then tied a pretty pink bow to the top brick in the faintly glowing pile. Inspecting his hands, Arnold noted that all seven fingers were still present and moderately functional. Excellent.

"Why, that should fool them nicely, love," his wife said as she hobbled up beside him. "Now let's get each other dressed for tonight. I wanna be outta here before any disgusting phants return." Mrs. Zigalot really did not like phants. Nobody did.

As his wife assisted him in the chore of sliding on his best patched T-shirt, Arnold reflected upon their lives together and their accomplishments. It was a brief contemplation. Arnold smiled contentedly, careful not to crack his lip again. By tomorrow, the phant pests would be gone. Life was so wonderful.

As twilight fell, a large assemblage of people shuffled and tottered around the brown lawn, trying mightily not to bump into and damage one another. It seemed that every *Homo sapien* in the neighborhood was attending. Others were interested in the goings-on, too. In fact, just over a nearby grassy hill, a shiny red puppy-sized figure with six spindly legs and two antennae peered slyly at the scene through an ingenious set of prisms. Stacked neatly next to her were a few leftover brown wax cartridges. On the front of each, in large bright blue letters, was stamped, "PARTY FOOD. HELP YOURSELF." Below this, in much smaller, ultraviolet type, was printed, "Poison. For human pest control only."

The phant lady groomed her antennae as she watched expectantly. The close vicinity of the humans made her multiple feet twitch.

She really did not like humans. Nobody did.

One Pink Unicorn, To Go

Max glanced up from his sleazy electronic video periodical as the front doorbell of J.M. Axtol, Inc. rang. A touch of the phase button on his desk and the view window in the door cleared, revealing a short, chunky gentleman wearing a plain yellow business suit and ordinary purple cape.

"Yes, may I help you?" Max asked cautiously.

The heavy, yellow-suited man looked acutely embarrassed. He coughed once, then said, "I understand that you manufacture...uh...exotic pets?"

Max relaxed and slid his finger to the right, dephasing the window to opaque while simultaneously opening the door. "Yes, indeed we do. Please come in." Max slipped a professional-looking veterinary periodical over his cheap magazine as the potential client stepped hesitantly inside. The street noises abruptly died as the door slid tightly closed.

Max lit his business smile and beckoned Yellow Man to the old-fashioned, cultured leather chair opposite his multi-functional plast-oak desk. The client glanced shyly around, then lowered himself gently into the offered seat. "You...make animals here?" he mumbled.

Handing the client a brochure, Max began his standard *schpiel*. "Sir, you have come to the right place. We here at J.M. Axtol, Inc. specialize in the manufacture of exotic DNA-coded genuine life forms. These items are living, breathing, eating organisms, and can be fashioned after a mixture of any known life forms, past or present. Of course," Max continued with a tight smile, "humanoid forms are strictly illegal."

"Of course."

Max continued now, ready for real business. "While all forms are released in their neonatal—that's "baby"—phase of development, we do have quite a few in stock which have been allowed to mature. Any size can be specified, but we create life forms on the premises only up to 5.7 cubic meters. Our subsidiary plant across town can vat-grow a life form of up to 10 cubic meters. Any larger living organisms require a city permit and the resources of the London Zoo. We don't make flying elephants here," Max added with a slightly patronizing chuckle.

The client grinned weakly back. "Oh, I don't want anything that big. I mean, I, uh, just was inquiring, uh, as to…well…"

"Why don't we take a look at some of our more recent products," Max interjected, touching the presentation button on his desk. A 3-D image of a six-legged lime green horse materialized comfortably in view of the client, romping through a field of electric blue daisies. As the animal turned toward the viewer and posed, it lifted two adjacent legs, revealing a large, round, suction-cup shaped foot pad on the end of each.

"Now this example is a real favorite with the kiddies. Featuring six extremities and double-jointed front pseudopods, this equine-based fantasy can run smoothly over the roughest terrain. The teeth are recessed into the gums—can't bite the baby! And note those foot appendages—patent held exclusively by J.M. Axtol, Inc.—this little gal can climb near-vertical walls!"

Max turned and bent forward to better scrutinize his client. "Well, what'cha think?"

"Oh, uh, gosh, that's very nice, but, uh…"

Max leaned forward in his faux-hide chair and flipped the continue switch. "I'm sure you'll be delighted to note that we have a large stock of many other genetic advances in embryonic cross-pooling. Here're just a few casual examples." The 3-D now displayed an orange-furred, toothless teddy bear, and then switched to a pair of butt-to-butt linked Siamese dachshunds, and then an eight-legged, three-tailed blue house cat. Something that appeared to be a cross between a miniscule leopard and a moth flitted quickly across the scene. A luminescent yellow beagle with small elephant ears and flippers jumped out of a pool, dropping a beach ball to gaze cutely out at the viewer. Max studied the client's evident lack of enthusiasm, and settled back to begin his "Smaller But Cheaper, Why Not Get Two" sales pitch. He tapped the "PLAN C-12" button and indicated the center of his desk as the 3-D faded from view.

As the plast-oak transilluminated, Max pointed enthusiastically into the brightly lit central cage now revealed under the surface of his desk. A 4-inch high perfectly proportioned Tyrannosaurus rex twisted its neck to leer up, a half-devoured cricket dangling loosely from its miniature jaws. "Just look at these monsters! Our ultra-mini-Tyrex has become quite a hit with the miniature hobbyists! And look at those teeth! This guy could bite your thumb off! Yet, when properly caged and regularly fed, this fellow is hardly more dangerous than a common rattlesnake was last century."

The yellow fellow stared. Max continued.

"All of our miniatures are based on reptilian chromosome patterns," Max pressed on. "We can grow small, exquisitely detailed replicas of most of the well-known dinosaurs." The various cages lit up in a consecutive pattern, showing brief glimpses of small, exquisitely detailed replicas of most of the well-known dinosaurs. The client blinked thoughtfully, but said nothing.

"And here's something very special," Max broke into the dead silence. "This is a whole new product line we have just started to explore." Max clicked yet another button, and a one-cubic foot opaque white box elevated out of the far corner of his desk. "Now don't startle him; he's really quite flighty," Max explained carefully as he touched a recessed control on his side of the box.

The client's jaw dropped open, and he emitted a quiet "Oh!" as a six-inch tall, pearl-white, beautifully shaped winged miniature horse stepped cautiously out onto the plast-oak, pawing the desk surface once and then looking about itself with slight unease. The pair of opalescent white wings on its back extended and then settled reluctantly into a parked position as the small Pegasus evaluated its surroundings.

Max felt the client's sharp interest and warmed up for the kill. "We based this unique demo model on years of research into many different genomes to get the incredible result that you see here before you. The process involved was extremely technical and of course highly classified, but what I can tell you is that we started with miniaturized Shetland pony genes and blended in a variety of traits that we felt would be desirable in a mythological animal. We utilized a particularly rare blend of canary DNA for the wing effect—quite stunning, don't you think?"

The client smiled hugely and reached out a quivering finger to stroke the downy-white equine back. The tiny winged horse turned its head, watching the finger suspiciously, and then let out a satisfied, but unfortunately very bird-like, chirp.

"Still a few bugs to be worked out!" Max flapped his hands to quickly herd the mini-beast back into its cubicle, shutting the door and jabbing the button to lower the creature back into the confines of the desk.

The client smiled again and began speaking. "I'm, uh, VERY interested in the mythological aspect of your, uh, well, I mean,…here, look at this." The man fumbled in his vest pocket, ultimately pulling out and unfolding a tattered square of yellowing paper. "This is what I, uh, want." He smoothed the aged paper onto the desk, sat back nervously, and waited.

Max scrutinized the illustration revealed on the document. "About what size is this organism to be at maturity?"

"Oh, uh, I'd say…four, five feet, or so,…to the head…"

"Hmmm…" Max pondered the illustration further. "Equine base, probably miniature would do, with…Is this forelock horn spiral? Yes? Any particular direction of rotation—clockwise, counterclockwise?"

"Uh…clockwise would be fine!"

"Any maturing to be done by us, or delivery at 'birth'?" Max continued.

"I just want a colt—I can be present then, can't I?"

"Sure, no problem—we can even have a ceremony, if you like. Now, how about sex?"

"What?" Client blinked myopically. "Oh, yes, uh...is neutered female available?"

"No problem." Max thought on. "Okay—equine base, mix in some goat horn genes—some narwhale elements would give that a nice spiral effect...Yes, this would be quite feasible." Max looked up and smiled again. "We could have this baby coded, initiated, and forced-rate vat-grown on our premises in about one month. Yes, exotic is our specialty. And you would be the first to own your own unicorn, hand-tailored to your private specifications." The first to have any such thing, really—this mythology set was a new field even for the geneticists, Max thought to himself, as he began summing up figures on his calculator.

"And now for the pricing. Let's see: life form permit, gene coding fee, replication fee, vat rental, conversion hours charges, untanking fee, tax, delivery—no delivery, that's right, you'll pick her up here. Oh, yes, let's just add in my tip. Okay, then, it comes out to...only eighty-nine thousand, nine hundred and ninety-five credits!" Max painted on a sincere, relaxed smile—no telling what this client's financial expectations might have been.

"Well, good, okay, and...Oh yes! Almost forgot!!" The fat client cautiously extracted a dark brown four-inch tall glass vial from his yellow coat pocket. "It's, uh, absolutely essential that, uh, this gets mixed in with the horn..." He set the vial gently on the counter. "Please be careful with this—it's, uh, really quite rare," he muttered, anxiety creasing his chubby facial features.

Max carefully slid the bottle towards himself. He lifted the glass stopper just a tad and peered inside. Rainbow-fluorescent hues glittered back at him, even in the truncated light reaching the inside of the dark vessel. "Exactly what is this stuff?"

"Well, uh, if you really must know..." the client sputtered a bit, then, closing his eyes, began reciting, "Eye of newt, uh, ear of bat, tail of frog, blood of horned lizard, three hummingbird feathers, five desiccated crocodile tears, the right-sided tongue of a two-headed serpent, and...uh...some other things, all finely ground and mixed in the shadow of the midnight arctic sun during a total eclipse. Oh, and, uh, the fresh cut hair from a 21-year-old virgin princess. Added, of course, just before the grinding stage."

"Of course." Max suppressed a snicker. "I suppose that last ingredient was the most difficult to find of all," he joked.

The odd man returned his gaze, without blinking. "Yes, it was." Max frowned as he slowly rolled the vial between his fingers. "And just what am I supposed to do with this?"

"Well, uh, I was thinking of just, uh, mixing it in...with the bones or something," the yellow man stated lamely. "Wouldn't that get some into the horn?"

"Not quite—horn is typically a skin derivative. Different germ cell layer." Max suppressed a groan as he came to the annoying realization that this client was a psycho. As an embryological problem, however, this puzzle was really quite fascinating, and Max continued to cogitate on a possible solution. Horn was derived from hair, which was derived from ectoderm...expose the embryonic neurulation stage to the concoction, carefully timed, sterile conditions of course....

"Oh! Oh! And the color! It...She...must be pink! The horn, the coat, everything...pink!!" The client shrank back into himself. "Any price would be worth paying. Anything. I've worked so long, so hard, for this...."

"Well, I understand, but getting into the vat with embryogenesis under way and putting in this—stuff—is really quite irregular, you know. We could never guarantee the result. And, of course, there is a minimum 25% fee for inanimate, rejected, or returned merchandise." Max leaned forward to catch the client's eyes. "It would have to cost a lot more, you realize."

"Two hundred thousand credits! I'll pay two hundred thousand credits! I have it here with me! Please, just try!!" Yellow man was almost sobbing.

Max rocked back in his chair. Two hundred thousand credits! And he was really soaking the crazy guy at 89,000! "Let me think some more."

Okay, add some pink canary genes...this time, make darn sure that no vocal genomes slip in...grown in a sealed vat, no light exposure until untanking...

"Yes, I do believe that we can do it!" Two hundred thousand credits...Max smiled, thinking of his commission. He loved making money, even from crackpots. "We can make your pink unicorn." As they finished shaking hands across the desk, both grinning broadly, Max continued, "85% down now, 15% upon delivery—I mean your pick-up here," Max amended quickly. "No ceremony, just a regular pick-up here would probably be best." With no chance to advertise a failure or mistake, Max thought. "For now, local bank draft, money order, or interplanetary credit card would be acceptable."

"I'd, uh, rather just pay it all now, if you, uh, don't mind." The client fumbled again in his coat pocket. "Ah, yes, here it is." He carefully counted out a number of green-printed worn paper rectangles onto the desk.

Max glared at the tattered pieces of paper. "What, may I ask, is that?" he demanded icily.

"I think they call it—cash."

"Cash? Oh yes! I'm sorry! I've just never seen it before—in person, you know. Just pictures in old 3-D's." Max studied the antique bills, then carefully inserted them into the universal ID analyzer slot built into his rather omnipotent desk. Machinery hummed, gears whirred, and a glowing green sign popped up out of the desk, adjacent to the slot. "TWO HUNDRED THOUSAND CREDITS CASH CURRENCY, VERIFIED" the sign blinked to Max.

"Great! Now we're just about done. If you'll kindly fill in these forms, current address and visiphone number, you know, I'll start right on your order today."

The client pecked slowly at the typing screen as he did the requested paperwork. Max stared at him. Maybe crazy, Max thought, but two hundred thousand credits was two hundred thousand credits—his commission could get him a new hovermobile, maybe a big sleek red one, or a weekend for three in the Antarctic Riviera...Max became aware that the client was finished with his form. Max took up the paperwork.

"Well, Mr.... Blackburn, I see...I'm certainly looking forward to seeing this pink unicorn myself," he said. Max pumped the client's eager hand one last time and led him to the door, depositing the man into the busy evening hover traffic. "J.M. Axtol, Inc. appreciates your business," Max concluded. "We will contact you in about four weeks for the final pick-up date and time for your selected life form. Have a pleasant month."

A white cubic four-foot diameter vat had been wheeled into his office and Max eyed it with certain trepidation. There was no way to know what was inside: the vat was sealed from early embryogenesis, just after Mr. Blackburn's "magic mixture" had been added. The artificial amniotic fluid had been drained this morning in the processing room, and all that remained to do was to break the door seal on the container to reveal what was hidden inside. Usually, this was the cheerful moment where the new life form met its new owner and everyone went away happy.

Today was a bit different, however. This vat allegedly held a grown fetus that had been tinkered with during embryogenesis. In his six years with the company, Max had encountered only three maturation failures, with one requiring immediate destruction. Max hoped fervently that this would not be a similar case.

Mr. Blackburn arrived precisely on schedule and excitedly hurried through the final paperwork. Max assisted him in cutting the plastic seal, and stepped back as the door on the vat swung open.

Both Max and the client gasped as they looked inside. Max was the first to speak.

"Uh—gosh! I'm sorry, but there appears to have been an, uh, unfortunate malfunction." Max turned to his client and added, "Gee, you know, there is that mandatory 25% service fee even when…"

"She's perfect! She's absolutely perfect!!"

"Uh…I don't see…well…is it? She is??" Max knuckled his eyes briskly and peered carefully back into the vat.

There was no mistake. The artificial umbilical stump hung limply from the far wall. He was correct in his first impression. The vat was otherwise completely, irrevocably—empty.

Max twisted his head sideways to better study his client, and thought very carefully before he spoke again. "You…really like her?"

"Oh, yes! She's so beautiful! Come here—come to Papa!" Mr. Blackburn caught Max's look, and stammered, "You—you—Are you a virgin?"

Max eyed the man in shocked disbelief. "Not since I was…young."

"I see." Mr. Blackburn blinked thoughtfully at Max one last time, then turned back to the vat, beaming from ear to ear, and held his arms out. After a moment, he seemed to be satisfied, and, while stroking thin air, spoke one last time to Max. "Is that all? Can I…we…go now?"

"Uh…sure. You're all paid up, and you have your, uh, property, and you can leave at any time. Please, go out the back door. Don't hesitate to call us for any questions." Or to call your shrink, thought Max.

As he ushered Mr. Blackburn and his imaginary friend out the rear exit, Max was left to ponder the diversity of human behavior and the ethics of monetary gain. He sighed, and turned back towards his desk. As he took a step, however, he slipped on something soft and wet on the floor.

"Hey! Wha'?" Max reached down to the floor and fingered a very wet, very warm, very soft, and quite invisible mass. He grabbed what he could of it and brought his apparently empty hand close to his face.

It smelled like horse manure.

It's a Jungle Out There

Sam lowered himself gently onto his arthritic knees. He carefully tugged on one thick leather glove as he eyed his immobile quarry. Slowly, carefully, he slid his protected hand towards the unsuspecting three-inch high green growth. With a quick pinch and tug, the culprit was pulled from the ground. Sam momentarily studied the saw-toothed leaves, the thorny stem, and the dangling root system. He dropped the plant with a satisfied mumble into the small trash bag at his side.

"One more weed gone," he muttered to himself, as he raised his gray-haired cranium to survey his garden. Brushing a few silver strands of hair from his eyes, Sam gazed fondly at the cherimoya trees, black sapotes, chocolate persimmons, blood oranges, and all the other exotic shrubs and trees in his private two acres of paradise. It had taken years of anguished patience to save up the cash in order to buy the small house far from the suburbs. His wife had greatly resented moving away from the city, away from her doting relatives and sarcastic friends. But Sam had been persistent in his wishes, and had bought the place, sold the apartment, and dragged his angry wife out to the isolated property. Now, after several more years of hard manual labor, his retirement dream of a peaceful, private garden utopia was close to a fact.

Sam loved working in the shade of the guava and banana trees, feeding his rare tropical fish in the little koi pond he had built two years before, and even enjoyed removing the stubborn tropical weeds inadvertently imported with his exotic flora. There had been so many big projects in the past to make his garden what he had envisioned, but they had all been accomplished. There continued to be hundreds of small tasks requiring his attention every day, but Sam enjoyed them all.

Sam's wife, Penelope, screamed at him from the inside of the nearby house. "Get inside now or lunch will be burned! I'm tired of your lazy loafing around out there!"

"Yes, dear!" Sam called back. He had devoted so many years to his wife, and now tried mightily to concentrate on the future and ignore her incessant demands and insults.

"I'm gonna get someone to cut down all of those stupid trees. I hate this filthy yard. Wall to wall concrete, that's easy to maintain. Not all of this dirt and idiotic jungle."

"Yes, darling."

"Take off your shoes! I won't have you tracking mud all over the house again."

"Of course, sweetness."

"And clean up that nasty wood pile in back! I've been after you for three years to get rid of that catastrophe! I'll bet it's full of spiders and who knows what else!"

"Yes, dear. After lunch, dear."

Sam smiled gently. Soon he would be able to clean up the house, lie in his hammock, and really relax. Sam slipped off his shoes as he trudged up the porch steps and into his house.

Sam wandered into the small kitchen, seating himself down across from his balding, housecoat-dressed wife, trying not to make eye contact across the cluttered kitchen table. He began spooning the ice cold vegetable-beef stew deliberately into his mouth.

"Did you get to that disgusting wood pile yet?" Penelope demanded.

"Not yet, honey. After lunch, I promise I'll take care of everything."

"We should've put concrete in. That's what Hazel did. She put in concrete. No plants, no bugs, no dirt."

"I like my trees, dear."

"Your trees! Your trees! It's always about your trees! I have a mind to get out there and burn down the lot."

Sam opened his mouth to say something, and then closed it. No sense in arguing—Penelope always got your goat, if she could argue with you long enough.

There was a cold silence. Then, "Where's the steak?"

"What, Penny precious?"

"Don't play dumb with me, you old fraud! I had to pull another T-bone out of the freezer. The one I had been defrosting is gone. If you're using it for fertilizer, Samuel, I'll make your life hell."

"Fertilizer? No, sweetheart, I would never do that."

Penelope continued to berate her indulgent spouse. "I don't know why the food is always disappearing around here. First the hot dogs from the deep freeze last month, then the hamburgers, and now this. And I've been watching you, Samuel. You've been sneaking out bits and pieces. I'll bet you're keeping an animal out there. I will NOT tolerate any mangy mutts skulking around the yard. I'll have you committed first. You know I can. I think you're going senile, and my friend Sylvia agrees. What do you have to say about THAT?"

"Whatever you say, dear." Sam smiled up at her, and then busied himself with his soup again. He had just hidden a big chunk of beef from the soup in his handkerchief, and stuffed it into his back pocket. In spite of her desperate accusations, Penny usually didn't catch him stealing food.

"You're not even touching your stew. If you're not gonna eat, then get to that wood pile!"

Yes. One big job left to do. Sam got up from the table, excusing himself to his spouse's sullen glare, slipped on his shoes, and slowly shuffled out the back door, into his garden.

He walked along the wood pile, now nearly eight feet tall and twenty feet long, stacked from the wall of the house and running out into the side yard. He thought it looked quaint, but Penny obviously did not agree. Because of the dense plantings, no one could see the wood or the house from the dirt road, anyway, even if someone chose to stroll out into this remote area. Sam began whistling to himself as he carefully stepped around behind the wood pile to examine his favorite acquisition.

Penelope never ventured out this far to see what he had hidden back here, which had always been just fine with Sam. But now his latest project had matured, and that changed everything. Sam knew instinctively that if he asked her nice, his wife would finally join him out here.

The bush was twelve feet tall, lushly foliated and a beautiful reddish green in color. Sam reflected back to three years earlier, when he had received the small mail-order package from Amazon Reclamation Industries, and how he had so meticulously germinated and then planted the enclosed seed in this carefully selected area. He recalled the long hours he had spent secretly watering and feeding the baby plant until it had grown into the gorgeous tree he now gazed upon so lovingly.

Sam glimpsed something near the base of his plant. He pulled a long stick from the wood pile, and carefully dragged the object towards himself. Stooping down, Sam picked up what was left of a T-bone steak, and noted approvingly the deep gnaw marks on the bone. No shred of meat or even gristle was left.

Sam grinned in anticipation. It appeared that things were right on schedule. He pulled out the piece of beef from his back pocket, and tossed it into the red-green foliage. There was a sudden snatch, and then a quick rustle among the branches, and the meat was gone.

One last job to do. Sam smiled gently, reaching again into the wood pile, and selected a stout, heavy branch. He whacked it experimentally into his palm. Then he called out to his wife.

"Penny, dearest, please come out here—I have something I want to show you."

The carnivorous plant let out a subdued belch. It sensed a new, big feeding today, and twitched its branches expectantly.

The Bard's Goldfish

I am writing you this letter very carefully because I have been cheated and I want to file charges. I have had a great injustice done to me, and I want you to be aware of all the details, so that you can more fully understand the enormity of my grief. You are not the first to receive this letter, but apparently no one else has had time or opportunity to answer me, so now you shall have your turn. I will start from the beginning.

I named him Herman, and he was the prettiest little goldfish you ever did see. He was exactly one and a quarter inches long, a very cheerful yellow-orange in color, and was always darting around the little round fishbowl I got him, always busy, and always happy.

Herman kept me company while I worked at home, typing up graduate manuscripts and the occasional high school report to meet living expenses. You see, I was waiting for my real job to materialize. Upon college graduation, I had applied to multiple professorships, at many prominent universities, but my coursework in the Humanities had allegedly not been specific enough for the work that I requested. Apparently the fields of English Literature and Philosophy were already filled up with full- and part-time instructors. On the phone, some secretaries mentioned a lack of a graduate degree or graduate school work, after college, but what did they know? If they were so smart, they wouldn't be mere secretaries, now, would they?

Of course, I had not been interviewed for any position in over six months, since the Government had been keeping track of me. I knew they kept tabs on the best and the brightest and they had kept me from getting a decent job because they were afraid of me. Afraid of my becoming well-known and respected, and advancing into some high level Government position, where I could expose their spying on me.

I have positive proof that they talked about me and plotted against me. Only a few minutes into each of my three job interviews last year, the phone would suddenly ring, and the interviewer would answer it (they always did!), and then he or she would say, "Excuse me, I have an emergency meeting now. I will be glad to meet with you at a later date. Please see my secretary for an appointment." But the promised follow-up interviews were always cancelled! Obviously, it was all a Government conspiracy to keep me in my little apartment, doing menial typing work, until I died.

Well, I wasn't too bitter. I knew how the game was played. I knew why old friends stopped visiting, and then stopped calling, and then changed to unlisted phone numbers. I knew why my neighbors stopped saying hello, and would stare at me from behind my back.

They were all terrified by my abilities, and my knowledge, and my incredible intelligence. Some of them undoubtedly were Government agents.

So I finally got Herman the goldfish for company. We got along very well, and he never called me names, or threatened to have me "committed," or anything of that sort. We were pals. I fed him his crushed goldfish flakes every morning at nine, and changed his water every Sunday at noon. Our friendship intensified and grew, right up until the accident.

It was a terrible accident—or was it? Could it have been deliberate? I'm beginning to think so. You see, I usually stored my carefully crushed and sifted "nerve pills," vitamin B6, in an old fish food container. Every morning, right after feeding Herman, I would add one-quarter level teaspoon of the vitamin to my breakfast noodles. I found that this nerve vitamin greatly increased my intellectual powers, and I reasoned that this would eventually help me to figure out a way to thwart the Government's plans to keep me unemployed.

What happened was that somehow the Feds found out about my nerve pills, and set a trap for me. They sent an agent into my apartment one night, and switched Herman's fish food jar with my B6 jar. They were so sneaky that I didn't notice the change at all for one whole month. Their deception finally dawned on me after I finally detected a fishy taste to my chicken-flavored breakfast noodles.

What alerted me to the switch was when I noticed that Herman was acting very strangely. He seemed more jumpy than usual, but I could detect no illness or other fish malady. I became concerned, and then frightened, before I finally comprehended the full scope of the food switch. Thinking about some spy breaking into my apartment to switch my nerve pills with goldfish food left me shaking in anger. They were very powerful, to be able to taunt me like that. But why harm an innocent little goldfish? It seemed so unfair.

I sat on the worn brown bean bag chair and stared at Herman for a long, long time. And in so closely observing him, I made my Great Discovery: Herman was darting back and forth in his bowl in a very special pattern.

It was Iambic Pentameter.

But try as I might, I could not understand the message!

I tried putting my ear next to the bowl, real tight, but heard nothing. I tried sealing my ear to the bowl with Vaseline, and then crazy glue, but that only hurt. Then I tried holding my head under water, in the filled bath, with Herman in the bath water too. After a few minutes, I thought that I could hear something, but the awkward and wet conditions prevented me from writing down more than a word or two.

So I did the next logical thing. After seeing an ad on the community bulletin board in the market, I called up some ten-year-old kid who wanted to sell his old used computer. I took my next month's rent, and bought it. I think that I got a really good deal. This ten-year-old even came up with a few encouraging tips. Unfortunately, I was too busy with my original plans to try putting electrodes from my ears into the fishbowl and into the wall socket.

My first attempt at placing the computer in the tub of water, and plugging it in, just resulted in fizzles and sparks, and left me afraid for Herman's safety. After drying the machine in the oven, I tried a simpler technique: I plugged an extra cable into an open port in the back of the computer, cut the cable, and placed the ends of the free wires into Herman's bowl. Then I turned the machine on.

At first, all I got on the screen was garbage. But after placing the fishbowl on a grounded aluminum cookie sheet, and wiring my toaster into the circuit, I was finally able to understand Herman!

He was writing Shakespeare.

Okay, not exactly what you studied in English Lit. 101, but close enough. The verses were highly original, being very fish-oriented, and with multiple references to water. I was able to get most of the words down in indelible marker on the backs of paper shopping bags before the prose flitted off the rapidly scrolling screen.

Herman, as I said, did not talk about what we normally talk about. After all, he was a goldfish. Instead, his verses concerned fishy things. And water, always water. Here's just one example:

> To swim, or not to swim
> That is the question.
> Whether 'tis nobler to sink
> Plummeting to the bottom, or to
> Rise to suck in foul, stenchy air
> It all, in the end,
> Is unfathom'ble.

Of course, I immediately wrote to multiple prominent university English departments, and then to many well-known literary clubs, and then to several respected national magazines, and then to a few select newspapers. Finally, I did get a response from the American Enquirer, and after a brief correspondence and one clandestine meeting the junior researcher that I met recommended that I speak with a very special and secret friend of his. He wrote down the phone number for me, and I did call, even making an appointment with Dr. Marvin Flechstein for the following week. I was very excited at meeting this psychiatrist, since I was informed that he had had years of training in understanding fish minds as well as the human kind.

Meanwhile, I was running out of clean paper bags, so I started cutting up boxes, and writing on these. The boxes were free from behind the market, and I cut the side panels into neat eight inch by eleven and one-half inch squares. I found the cardboard rectangles to be very convenient, as well as more durable, especially when frequently dealing with water.

Finally, with fish bowl cradled gently in one arm and cardboard documents under the other, I visited Dr. Flechstein's office. He called me in, eventually, and listened attentively to every detail of my story. Then he started asking awkward questions about my education, and then about my mother, and then things got very angry. I left in a big huff, quickly grabbing up my cardboard notes as I rushed out.

I must have been quite agitated, all those inexplicable sexual questions and all, because I accidentally left Herman in Dr. Flechstein's office! I tried several times in the next few days to get back in, and rescue my goldfish, but the doctor never was there when I arrived, and eventually the office itself was locked up.

Naturally, I became more depressed than ever, so I lay screaming in bed for several days. Finally, I became so angry at Them (I won't say Who anymore, because They are listening) that I decided to go and get another goldfish, and see if I could train him to write the Great Bard as I had trained Herman.

My new goldfish, Humphrey, was ready, and willing, but I guess my heart really wasn't in it, and all I ever got out of him was cheap rhyming verse.

Then, at the end of the month, I ran out of noodles, and walked dejectedly to the local mini-market to buy another year's supply. But in the convenience store magazine rack I saw a picture that shocked me more than my first job rejections had.

A familiar face leered out from among the magazine covers. Not on the cheap trashy pulp, not even on the American Enquirer, but on real, respectable magazines, including Timely, Persons, and True Detective. I picked up a copy of Newspeak and read the blaring headline above the familiar, smirking picture: "THE NEW SHAKESPEARE? PSYCHIATRIST MARVIN FLECHSTEIN'S LATEST LIQUID PROSE ASTOUNDS THE EXPERTS!!!"

I ran home with my noodles and sat down and started writing to influential people. Needless to say, I have been cheated, and I hope that this letter sheds some light on Dr. Flechstein and his amazingly sudden grasp of English literary verse. I think that you should call for an investigation, and arrest this phony psychiatrist, and confiscate all of his possessions.

I want my goldfish back.

That Time of the Month

Sultan Azi bin Wheezer Nebbish threw the ivory grape spoon with a splintering crash to the marble floor of his bedroom.
"WHERE IS OUR TWENTY-SEVENTH WIFE?" he thundered.

Grand Vizier Tuchus cringed under the tirade. He pulled a sheaf of papers out from beneath his gown, and licking his finger, leafed through the pile. Shortly he paused, scanned a line, matched a column, and muttered an obscurity to himself. He rescanned and rematched before regretfully intoning, "She is unavoidably detained at this time, Your Excellency."

"Doing what?"

The Grand Vizier tentatively stepped up to the elevated loveseat of the Sultan's bedroom. "I'm terribly sorry, Sir," he whispered, "but she...the female...It's that time of the month, you know."

The Sultan dropped his ponderous head to his fleshy hand, and cradled his sweaty brow in the thick fingers. "Just how long must we wait for this to be over?"

"Well...you know...it's usually about, uh, up to one week?"

"We cannot wait one week!"

"Then there is a problem...."

The Sultan glared anew at his most trusted Vizier, who seemed incapable of carrying out His Majesty's simplest wishes. To be politically correct, however, Sultan Nebbish decided to be diplomatic.

"Where is our wife number twenty-six?"

Grand Vizier Tuchus reconsulted his Royal Mating Tables in earnest. Unfortunately, what he had been fearfully anticipating for months, had finally come to pass. Tuchus sighed deeply. "The same problem, My Lord."

"Wife number twelve?" The Sultan had a preferential list of most favored wives, and he was prepared to backtrack all the way to wife number one if the situation demanded it. Well, maybe wife number three.

Tuchus skipped through his tables, muttering to himself, and finally sighed with the inevitable acceptance of Wiley Coyote seeing the anvil zooming down towards his head. "I'm afraid not, Your Superiorness."

"Number nineteen? Five? Fifteen? Any of the low twenties?"

The Grand Vizier folded his arms, lifted his chin, and fixed his gaze upon a green Ming urn spittoon. "It appears," he intoned as calmly as he could, "that, unfortunately, all of your beautiful, intelligent, uh…adoring wives are, um,…clinically predisposed."

"You mean that we cannot fulfill our manly duties? To any of them?"

Tuchus straightened as best he could under the glaring gaze of his leader. "Yes, Your Eminence, it does appear that a short period of abstinence is in…"

"YOU WILL FIND ME AN ACCEPTABLE ALTERNATIVE AT ONCE!" Sultan Azi ben Wheezer Nebbish had become so flustered, he forgot to maintain his royal pronoun plurals. Such insubordination was a shock to his entire system.

Grand Vizier Tuchus cleared his throat nervously as he absorbed the outburst. "Your Royal Majesty," he intoned, "you know the law better than any of your loyal subjects."

Sultan Nebbish glared quizzically at his advisor. After all, he was Sultan, and he could glare in any manner he chose.

Tuchus closed his eyelids gently and recited, "No more than one bride per quarter. No manly administrations prior to marriage vows. And," he added sternly, forcing his gaze to meet the Sultan's eyes, "No hanky-panky with any woman during her time of the month!"

Sultan Nebbish sighed in defeat, trying mightily not to pout. Here he was, the greatest leader of recent history (as his advisors so often reminded him), yet he was unable to satisfy his male urges, which he most desperately needed to do.

"Hokay," he sighed, "so how long must we wait?" Stifling his indignation, the Sultan was able to shift back to proper royal plural pronoun.

Tuchus suppressed a mutter and once again pulled out the Royal Mating Schedule. "Ummm...yes...okay...." The vizier looked up and meekly smiled. "In exactly five days, all will be back to normal, and you shall have your, uh, pick. Sir."

"THAT IS TOTALLY UNACCEPTABLE TO US!" Gathering up his bulk, the Sultan stood up pontifically and stamped his ample foot. "BRING US THE ROYAL ASTROLOGER."

Within minutes, the Royal Astrologer had arrived, huffing and puffing and all out of breath. "Yes, Sir, Your Eminence, Sir?" he pleaded, surreptitiously brushing double nutty fudge cookie crumbs from the lap of his austere white professional gown.

The Sultan had by now calmed himself down, and was settled again in the pink stuffy loveseat. He addressed the skinny man with great royal patience. "I have a teensy little problem," he began. Coyly eyeing the squirming fortune teller, he carefully considered how best to articulate his immense and unfulfilled hormonal desires. He kept it short.

"Our women are all on their period. We want to have sex. Now."

The astrologer was caught completely off guard and shock registered on his usually serene features. "Oh, uh, well...I have two very faithful wives, and, uh, well, I have never, uh, with a man, and, uh...."

The Grand Vizier rushed up to the dangerously confused astrologer and whispered something urgent into his waxy ear.

Brightening considerably, the astrologer smiled up at the Sultan, and let out a subdued, "Oh! With a woman! Well, that's a relief!" Then, assuming a more demonstrative stance, and stroking his goatee thoughtfully, he studied the backs of his eyelids for a moment before making an Announcement.

"I must consult the charts!" And he whirled and exited the bedroom.

"Ah, nuts," muttered the Sultan. Then, "We have thought heavily upon this subject, and we feel that the services of the Grand Master Magician are required."

Grand Vizier Tuchus was so shocked that he nearly dropped the girlie magazine which he had just pilfered from the Sultan's golden nightstand. "But, Sir, the Grand Master Magician...You've had him locked up in the Black Tower for nearly two months! Uh, in your extraordinarily wise way, of course, Sir."

His Highness deigned to smirk. "We have forgiven him. Bring him forth to us."

"But, Sir," continued the stricken vizier, "he turned Prince Rasine, twenty-third in line for the throne, into a goat!"

"A golden goat! Yes, very impressive, indeed."

"But Your Highness..."

"STOP BLEATING AND DO AS WE COMMAND!!"

Grand Vizier Tuchus shuddered inwardly, but clapped his hands, and one of many concealed but ever-present bedroom guards ran to do the Sultan's bidding.

In a very short time, which could only be possible in a feudal state with an omnipotent overlord, the recently imprisoned Grand Master Magician Dewoony was brought in chains before Sultan Azi bin Wheezer Nebbish. A once dignified robe of glistening black, adorned with pearly-white crescent moons and five-pointed stars, had been reduced to tatters. Torn Hawaiian print bikini underwear could be seen through the holes in the seat of the robe. Heavy metal wrist cuffs and anklets weighed down the scrawny limbs of the now gibbering Master Magician.

Sultan Nebbish reluctantly eyed the fallen magician with royal misgivings. Maybe he had been a little bit harsh with that goat thing. "We welcome you back to civilization!" he congratulated Magician Dewoony.

"Grrrr..." was the reply.

"Hmmm?" The Sultan fluffed a pillow and resettled himself on his pink loveseat. "Now where were we? Oh, yes! Guards, remove the chains, please. And a new robe. A rabbit lined darkish one will do, we believe."

The Grand Master Magician blinked rapidly as his hands and feet were freed, and his worn rags covered by comfy finery. Yes, feudal monarchies did lend credit to speed.

"Now, Mister, um, Master Magician, we have a problem that we truly believe you alone have the power to fix. You will agree to help us, hmmm?" The Sultan cast his brooding eyes down and found an offensive hangnail to worry.

After an explanation of the Sultan's current dilemma was discretely delivered to Dewoony, the magician's eyes began to glitter and a crooked grin split his thin white beard. "Yeah? Heh, heh, heh. No problem. But I will need my magic wand, of course. The crimson one."

Sultan Nebbish waved a chunky hand and a nervous guard was dispatched to fetch the desired object. Upon the guard's return, the magician snatched it up, with just a little chortle of glee escaping his cracked lips.

The Sultan sat up in his loveseat, and composed himself. "You may start," he commanded.

"Your wish is my command!" giggled the newly freed Master Magician. He briefly scratched himself in an effort of concentration. Or maybe it was just an itch. Then he began.

"Stooble pooble gooble!" he chanted, and waved his arms in a curious little pattern. A little line of spittle dripped from one corner of the excited magician's mouth.

"Oogle floogle, on oogle noogle!" The wand began to glow.

"Slingus muddus, ingus puddus," Magician Dewoony continued. He leaned toward the cowering Grand Vizier. "That means, 'What goes around, comes around,'" he sniggered in a stage whisper.

"Ripple poodle, changus droodle, NOW" and with a sharp clap of his gnarled hands, a brilliant red glow suffused the room. As the bright light faded, it became apparent that the Master Magician had vanished.

"Well," the Sultan made an effort and wiped a pained expression from his face, "that's that." He dabbed a bead of sweat from his brow, and self-consciously fiddled with the pink pillow of his loveseat. The handful of royal guards and the Grand Vizier remained still and uncertain of what to do or say.

Moments later, a harem eunuch exploded through the harem door and bowed himself into the great royal bedroom.

"Your Excellency! Sir! Please excuse the intrusion! Your immediate services are desired by your wives!!"

"Oh? Of which wife do you refer?" The Sultan allowed a bemused smile to touch his chubby face.

"Why, all of them, Sir! They are drawing lots even as we speak, to see who gets you first!"

"Aha! You see?" the Sultan glared meaningfully at his Grand Vizier. "This silly monthly female clinical thing has been ended by our Master Magician. You will see, our kingdom will be grateful."

Gathering himself up, Sultan Nebbish stood and waddled across the room towards the open harem door. "We will call upon you later. Or maybe on Tuesday," he yelled over his shoulder to his trusty Vizier as he squeezed through the door. A faint chorus of high-pitched giggles came from beyond his bulk. The polished, gold-encrusted, oak door swung shut behind him with what sounded like an anticipatory sigh.

Later that night, the great and mighty and thoroughly exhausted Sultan Azi bin Wheezer Nebbish shuffled down his royal hallway. Too much, too soon, he thought as he tried to massage his aching lower back. He felt tired, nauseous, and bloated, and was beginning to develop a nasty headache.

Just then the Royal Astrologer came crashing around a corner, pursued by two royal guards. They tackled him just as he spotted the Sultan.

"Horrid! It's horrid!" he sobbed as they dragged him bodily away. "Mars and Venus have subconjugated! My charts are ruined!! It's horrid!!" The struggling group disappeared around the corner, the loyal guards finally removing the irrational man from the delicate sight of the Sultan, who had regally chosen to ignore the entire spectacle.

Sultan Nebbish scratched his head and again rubbed his back. Well, after a good night's sleep, and a long massage, he'd feel much better, he reflected. And now, maybe a little bladder assuagement was in order.

So thinking, the Sultan led himself into the royal urinal room, and proceeded to unzip and relieve himself in the appropriate imperial receptacle. After rubbing his cramping back, Sultan Nebbish fumbled to refasten his silken pants, glanced down, and stopped. Looking down. Into the urinal.

He had just peed out a significant quantity of blood. With little clots.

Sultan Nebbish awkwardly came to the startling revelation that this might just be the beginning of an uncomfortable monthly occurrence for a long, long time to come.

A Little Hair Transplant

In the midst of a bitter cold, dusky mid-winter evening, the two strangers came knocking at the back-alley door of my little medical clinic.

"Good evening," I said as I discretely let the muscular man and his slender, hooded companion into my outer office, closing the front door carefully behind them. "How may I help you?" Having just flunked out of a not-too-choosy medical school, and not having any real credentials to practice medicine (or license), I was very careful to size up all customers for possible State Medical Board investigators.

"Saw your ad in the Daily Sun," the man explained in a thick New England accent. "Have a problem. Need your opinion. Kept confidential?" The last was more demand than query.

"Sure. Tell me what you need, and I'll see what I can do."

Neither of these two characters looked the least bit like the stuffy bureaucratic board investigators I was so cautiously avoiding. The slender, hooded figure appeared too dainty for such demanding work, and the man…what were those horny bumps projecting from his temples?

The strange man continued, unhurried. "Need your promise of absolute secrecy. Anything seen or heard must be told to no one."

I leaned a little closer to the stranger and stared him squarely in the eye. "No medical records. No paperwork. You got the cash, I fix the problem." Which was pretty much true. I never wrote anything down, kept no medical records, and never, ever discussed my not-strictly-legal activities with anyone. Maybe I wasn't such a hot doctor, but there were plenty of people willing to seek me out for all kinds of private ills.

The man flashed a crooked smile. "I see we talk the same language," he murmured. "I got cash," and he exposed a huge wad of bills. "And I got one small problem." He indicated his friend. "But first some preparations. Got an exam room?"

"Yes, sir, right this way. If you could just give me some idea of the problem, I'm sure that I could..."

"Bald spots."

"Oh, I see." And I realized that this man's silent comrade must be the object of my exam as that hooded figure slithered by me. Noting this figure to be femininely petite and very curvaceous in all the right places, I guessed that a balding female "significant other" would be a good cause for discretion.

"No, you stay here." And the stranger blocked my movement into the exam room with one large, well-manicured hand. "Need to use a mirror."

Now, I recall reading about how ancient physicians in the Orient had had to examine ladies by palpating replica dolls, but I had never been presented with this twist. Then I remembered that big roll of bills in the stranger's pocket. "No problem," I agreed amicably.

The man reached over to his covered associate, who now stood hidden behind the half-open doorway of the exam room. He held up a small mirror to let me view his friend. With one hand he tipped off the hood which hid her face, then leaned back, angling the mirror so that I could see the reflection.

Now I've had some severe shocks in my life. As a child, not being able to find my pet bunny Fluffy, while Ralph the dog had an upset tummy and fur caught in his teeth. Or being told on my eighteenth birthday that I had been adopted off the black market. Or on prom night, back in high school, finding out my sultry prom date was really another guy in drag.

This was a shock of another magnitude. This lady had snakes in her hair.

No, not in her hair, they WERE her hair. Then I recalled some tidbit of Greek mythology, about a similar case of a lady with snakes for hair. How anyone looking directly at her face was turned into stone.

The mirror trick was starting to look like a good idea.

"Uh-huh. Hmmm." I made some serious doctor noises as my thoughts spun around. Refocusing my eyes on the mirror, I forced myself not to panic, but to study the snake head more carefully.

There were one, two, no, three spots where individual snakes had apparently withered and died, resulting in bare patches on this lady's scalp. Her face actually was very pretty, but the snakes were live, hissing softly, and wriggling with subdued vigor now that they were freed from their encasing hood.

The snakes actually were rather attractive, I thought, being thankful that I had always had an affinity for their kind. Their colors were nice, most of them being a muted iridescent red or orange hue, and they did not seem overly aggressive. Some of them eyed me back in the mirror, flicking their sensitive tongues in and out, possibly wondering what plans I was formulating.

"Well," I began. Then, "Well." How does one grow snakes on their head? Did they hatch from eggs, or were they born live? Were these special snakes, adapted to stay fixed in one spot, or did they grow, what did they eat, and how were they connected to this lady's head? Was she a type of snake? The questions seemed to be endless, and I was rapidly becoming mentally overwhelmed with this case.

Then I became aware of my peculiar predicament. What if I didn't deliver? Would I forfeit my soul, or merely be turned into a plaster statue?

Forcefully shifting gears, I blanked out my panicked questions, and tried to think like a dermatologist. Hair was hair. Hair could be transplanted. Hair could be moved from one spot to another. Could hair be added on? Why not?

Once my thinking was reoriented, I found that the answers slipped neatly into place. Where to get more snakes? From the pet shop. How to attach? Needle and thread, with a general anesthetic for the snakes and a local anesthetic for the lady. How to deal with the other snakes already there? Knock them out with chloroform. How to avoid turning myself into a rock? Get a pair of spectacles modified with prisms and blinders, so that all images were reflected. What to charge for my services?

"This may cost quite a bit," I said, trying to keep my eyes from shifting down to the man's pocket full of dough.

"I'll pay $20,000 up front, and $80,000 upon completion." Attempting to cover my surprise at the large sum offered, I looked at my watch, and thankfully noticed how late it was. "I'll need to obtain some, uh, supplies," I stated cautiously.

"Here's the advance." The man must have figured me out early on. He handed me part of the wad of cash. "Get what you need. Will return tomorrow morning, say at seven?"

"Sure, seven." The advance money vanished into my coat pocket as I silently watched the now re-hooded Medusa and her escort slide out the entrance. Preparing a mental check list, I began closing up shop. A quick visit to an optician friend for the specialized glasses, then to the pharmacy for chloroform for the snakes, and finally an early a.m. pick-up at the pet store, and I would be ready. I hoped.

Things actually went much smoother than anticipated. I got the glasses ("for a new 3-D video game," I told the optician), picked up three very pretty snakes, and snuck into my alley entrance early. At seven a.m., right on time, the stranger and his exotic girlfriend showed up at the alley door.

They seemed to be pleased with my choice of snakes and equipment. After preparing the patient and her resident snake harem, using my special prismatic glasses, I managed to attach the anesthetized pet shop snakes to my client's head. It really wasn't that hard at all, just cut off the snake tail immediately distal to the caudal plate, suture the nerve root and vessels onto the neurovascular bundles which I exposed in the center of each bald spot on the lady's head, and then stitch the snakeskin bases to surrounding anesthetized snakes. It was quite simple, really, and before I knew it, we were done, the unusual couple had left, and I had a huge sum of money in my pocket.

After this, Sylvia (that was the Medusa lady's name) would come by about once a month for check-ups, and we stumbled into a somewhat unusual business arrangement. Since the Medical Board had finally caught me and closed me down, and I was looking for a new line of work anyway, Sylvia came up with a neat partnership idea. She would supply the raw material, and I would continue my monthly checkups on her "hair."

Well, now that I'm out of the medical racket, I find that I have much more leisure time, and my new exotic statuary business is really booming. I'm making more dough than I ever dreamed possible, and my artwork is seen in all the best hotels, luxury homes, and even a few museums.

Although Sylvia and I have developed a good professional relationship, we have never really become close friends. And although we meet frequently to talk over business, there are two subjects which we do not discuss. I never ask her where she gets those beautiful, perfectly formed, life-like statues, and she never quizzes me why I insist on carrying a mirror or two whenever we meet.

Tough Guys

Sitting behind the relative safety of his plain gray metal-sculpt desk, Tony called for the next individual in the long line of fierce and angry applicants.

"Next," he chimed, tunelessly, fiddling with the dials on his desk-mounted info screen.

A burly, dusky man with small curved tusks projecting meaningfully from beneath his snarling upper lips stomped up. The metal studs in his pseudo-leather collar glistened in the bright lights of the enormous gymnasium. He spoke.

"I am Chud the Conqueror. I am here to win your tournament," the tough looking character rumbled with a very rough accent. There he paused, making Tony look up.

"That's fine, Mr. Conqueror," Tony said. "Continue. Or haven't you had a chance to review the brochure?"

Chud dropped his blood-shot horn-rimmed eyes in embarrassment to the floor.

"Chud the Conqueror not a reader," he mumbled.

"No problem," Tony said in a soothing voice. "Let me read it to you, and then you can answer the questions, okay?"

Chud didn't appear to change his expression. Tony sighed, picked up the top pamphlet of a pile neatly stacked on his desktop, thumbed it open, and began reading.

"Welcome to the Sixth Intergalactic Toughest Organism Contest. Please insert your Identicard into the labeled desk slot in the Registration Desk upon entry into the combat gymnasium. This card must already be updated with all pertinent information, including your home planet and intergalactic mailing address, IG standardized age, any special physical challenges which you may have, and the official name of your usual combat style."

Tony glanced up. "You have heard all this before, yes?"

Chud furrowed his brows for a few thoughtful moments, and then nodded. Tony continued.

"Upon arrival at the Registration Desk, please answer all questions asked by the Official Registrar seated there. Be sure to speak slowly and clearly in Intergalactic English into the microphone in front of you. All statements will be recorded using standard audio-video-vibratory-olfactory equipment. The entry fee is sixty glutons, and must be deposited in person. This fee will only be accepted at the Registration Desk upon initial presentation of the combatant to the tournament. For security purposes, you must remain a minimum of three meters from the Registration Desk at all times, until it is your turn to register."

Tony glanced up at the massive combatant. Chud stared thoughtlessly ahead for a moment, then, dropping his gaze to his feet, slipped away from the desk a few more centimeters. Tony continued.

"At the Registration Desk, you will find a trained bureaucrat who will officially register you and help you with any questions about the tournament. However, please note that this Registrar is not responsible, nor does he have any interest in, any problems concerning your accommodations, meals, environmental controls, or anything else not directly associated with registering you for this contest. Please refrain from damaging this individual. Any physical attacks upon his person will be immediately and severely punished."

Tony glanced up at Chud to make sure he was still attentive. Then he resumed reading.

"You may study the three thousand nine hundred and forty-two-page liability disclaimer at your leisure and anytime prior to the initiation of your first melee. This liability form must be signed and witnessed, however, before you will be allowed into the contest ring with any of your opponents."

Tony finished and looked back up at Chud the Conqueror.

"Do you understand these directions?" he asked.

Bloodshot eyes had dimmed quite a bit during the long oratory. With the final question, however, Chud jerked upright and bared his tusks in a porcine smile.

"Chud now ready to fight. Is this trophy?" he drooled as he gazed longingly at the elaborately sculpted gold- and platinum-plated eighteen-inch high object just to Tony's left. The engraved gold plate at the base of the gaudy thing stated proudly, "The Winner."

Tony glanced over at the glittery statue. "Why, yes, this is the First Place trophy," he agreed. "But you would never guess what the Grand Prize is." Reaching over and gently prying the identicard from Chud's twitching three-clawed hand, Tony inserted it into his desk slot and typed a few entries into the info screen.

"Your files appear to be in order. Please deposit sixty glutons at this time," he said.

The Conqueror awakened from his inspection of the glimmering award and deposited the requested denominations. On cue, a briefly clad husky female wearing pseudo-leather with lots of metal studs appeared and escorted the dour combatant away.

"Next," Tony called.

A very thin and delicately contoured pink fairy-like thing with glistening quatrefoil wings flitted up to the Registration Desk. A soprano voice twittered out a greeting.

"Hi, big guy," the fairy-thing said, as he (?) delicately inserted his personal identicard into the appropriate desk receptacle.

"Good morning," answered Tony, scanning the information on the info screen. "Hmmm. This says that your usual method of attack is poison?"

The fairy-thing parted its lips to expose six opposing pairs of needle-like incisors, glistening with some yellowish milky substance.

"That is correct."

"For the record, and you must answer truthfully or face disqualification, are any toxic compounds utilized by yourself at any time during your combative maneuvers in any way artificially enhanced to increase their deleterious effects on opposing combatants?"

The fairy-thing smiled again. A drop of the milky-yellow stuff dripped out and hit the floor with a soft sizzling sound.

"No."

"Good answer. Sixty glutons, please." Tony waited for the deposit, finished the paperwork, and then verbally summoned the next critter in line.

"Next, please."

"I'm already here, ya big lout," said a small, tinny voice.

The Registrar looked around, but the next applicant in line was impatiently waiting the required three meters away, and had not yet spoken. The voice Tony heard was definitely coming from directly in front of him, so he addressed his next remarks to the air in front of his desk.

"I'm sorry. Full invisibility has been disallowed this year as an overly unfair advantage in sparring."

"Look down in front of your obese desk, ya stupid sop. I'm standing right here in plain sight, or are ya blind as well as retarded?"

Tony stood up and leaned over the top of the large desk, and located the source of the insults.

"Hmmm. You're a scrappy little guy, aren't you?" A one-half inch caterpillar-like alien being was barely visible standing (reclining?) in front of the desk. He raised his front one-quarter inch and argued angrily back at the Registrar.

"You fat Voltarian pig! We, the Cutinky people, are the strongest organisms per unit weight in the known universe! We can lift over ten-thousand times our own weight! Just because the rest of you are fat and clumsy doesn't mean that we should be excluded from these games." The worm thing was clearly agitated.

"Now, that's very nice," agreed Tony soothingly, "but couldn't you be rather easily trod upon by one of the more massive beings such as those you see around you? You know my primary purpose here as the Official Registrar is to make certain that no significantly unfair advantage, or disadvantage, is realized by any one individual contestant. Quite frankly, your small size places you at such an apparent disadvantage that I really ought to disqualify you. I'm sorry."

The worm puffed itself out to twice his initial size, or about the mass of a peanut. "You dirty bastard! You piece of Sorkan drip-drool! You watch and see just how powerful I can be!"

So saying, the worm bug crawled surprisingly quickly over to the closest desk leg, and lifted it slowly and shakily over its body. That corner of the desk lifted grandly all of a half-inch from the floor.

Tony was impressed. "That is impressive!" he suggested. "Tell me, though, just how long can you continue to lift such an incredible weight?"

"About...ten...seconds...."

"Oh, really? But you've been holding up that corner of my desk now for at least that long, haven't you?"

"You are...correct!" And with that final word, the worm thing must have gotten all tired out, because the heavy desk bumped back down to the floor, with a small squishing sound barely audible in the noisy room. A tiny puddle of greenish liquid pooled out from beneath the corner desk leg. Tony sat back down in his chair and typed an entry onto the info screen.

"Next."

A heavily armored lobster-like thing grunted and thudded forward.

"I be Vladimir, the Scimitar-Wielding Fiend of Three Planets," the lobster thundered, very melodramatically. "I be the greatest beast-killer of all time and in all of history. I be..."

"Why, that's fascinating!" Tony interjected. He already felt a smidgeon of repulsion for the supreme arrogance of this being. "Please tell me, as a devout student of martial arts history, just how many beasts have you killed? The grand sum total, if you don't mind."

"I be the most-foul murderer of a total of one thousand, two hundred, fifty-seven living beings, and I be the injurer of two thousand and four bleeding things."

"Wow, that's just incredible!" Tony smiled. "But you must remember, of course, that those numbers make you the SECOND worst killer and maimer in history."

"Eh?"

"I'm terribly sorry, but I do recall that among ancient human records, a man named Theogenes of Greece was credited with single-handedly killing one thousand eight hundred humans, and injuring a total of two thousand one hundred and two, using an unarmed method of physical combat known as the pancratium." Tony sighed, feigning deep regret. "We're a mite short of those numbers, now, aren't we?"

Lobster boy stood very still as he digested this tidbit of information. Then, with a horrendous roar, he raised his quivering and massive exoskeletal claws and focused in on the Registrar, sitting placidly behind his desk.

The horrible lobster creature spoke one last time, preparing his attack. "I now kill one thousand two hundred and fifty eyyyy...."

The last shouted word, of course, was cut short as the massive lobster torso fell through the secret trapdoor remotely triggered by the Registrar. The final syllable quickly faded into oblivion as the lobster-man slid down a long tunnel into the interspecies pokey below.

"Read the brochure," Tony muttered. "Nobody attacks the bureaucrat." The trap mechanism clicked back in place, and the next candidate floated up.

Floated, as in bright-orange glowing plasma cloud of superheated energy, measuring maybe one foot in diameter and roughly spherical. The glowing blob pulsated faintly.

"I yam here for tournamen." The accent was strong but the message understandable.

Tony reflected carefully on the nature of the creature. "Present your identicard, please."

"Hit burned hup." There was a trace of remorse in glowball's tone.

"Interesting." The Registrar stroked his chin in thought. "And what is your style of combat, please?"

"Incinerhation."

Tony sat back. "How original. You realize, of course, that incineration, flame, plasma, and other forms of high-enthalpy defense have been voided this year due to that regrettable spectator incident during the Fifth Intergalactic Toughest Organism Contest?"

"Hoh, really?" The glowing plasma ball faded to a much duller orange in disappointment.

Being the trained bureaucrat that he was, Tony had a solution.

"Of course," he continued, "you can always enter the First Interspecies Zoned-out Zero Limitation Exposition." Then, in an apologetic voice, "Sorry, but I didn't come up with that particular acronym." Tony continued in a helpful tone of voice, "It is my understanding that F.I.Z.Z.L.E. is a multispecies group of warriors formed very recently to allow high-enthalpy beings such as yourself and other individuals not easily accommodated by contests supporting protoplasm-based limitations, to get together and blast one another to oblivion. Here's their info pamphlet."

The paper immediately burned up as the fireball touched it, of course, but the creature did not seem to notice. "Sero limitation hexposition? Hoh, goody!" And the organism floated off on a draft of hot air towards the exit.

"Next."

Just then a sharp crackle sounded as a glimmering circular window appeared in the space immediately in front of the Registration Desk. An amplified, confident voice rang out.

"Greetings, weak beings of the insignificant matter-filled universe. We are here to claim victory in your pointless tournament."

Tony scratched his ear and regarded this apparition in bemused surprise. The message continued with a reverberating P.A. speaker effect.

"We of the superior anti-matter universe have developed a hero of such great physical strength, beauty, and *chutzpah*, that we know without a doubt he could single-handedly defeat all opposing organisms in your puny matter universe without even sweating much."

Tony's reply was only a touch on the defensive.

"Fascinating. Matter verses anti-matter. A very unique combat approach. But, I must theorize—please correct me if I'm wrong—wouldn't it be true that the interaction between your anti-matter hero and our regular-matter universe would result in such a horrendous explosion that not only this gymnasium, but the planet it is on, and in fact most of this star system, would be completely demolished? That there would be nothing left useful to conquer in this quadrant of space?"

The opaque window shuddered in a very self-righteous manner, as the patronizing voice continued. "That is why we should win by default. But we tire of this pointless debate. Our greatest military minds are personally observing this present transaction, and we all concur that your ugly universe must be thoroughly cleansed of yucky matter things anyway. We plan to momentarily launch an invasion force of brave and superior anti-matter organisms into your wimperingly weak universe of treacherous matter. We merely require you to concede defeat before we go on to clear your annoying universe of your disgusting protoplasmic stench." The anti-matter window quivered with symbolic arrogance.

Tony was not visibly upset. "You mean, you want to be declared winners of our little contest, and then you plan to destroy us?"

"That is the way it has always been with the incredibly strong and the intractably weak. You must do as we say. Logically, you have no reasonable alternative."

Tony scratched his head momentarily, and sighed.

"Well, then, I guess your anti-matter universe wins the prize."

"Of course we do. It is the only obvious conclusion," boomed the loud, grandstand voice.

"Okay. Here's the prize!" Tony picked up the heavy golden trophy next to him and chucked it easily through the opaque circular porthole into the alternative universe. There was an incredibly brilliant flash and then the window simply disappeared as the dense matter object interacted with the local anti-matter of the other universe in what must have been one mother of a multi-megaton explosion.

"Oops." The Registrar blinked thoughtfully at the sudden clearing of the anti-matter window from the room. Leaning down to his deepest bottom desk drawer, out of view of any contestants, Tony pulled out an elaborately sculpted gold- and platinum-plated eighteen-inch high statue. The engraved gold plate at the base of the gaudy thing stated proudly, "The Winner." There were easily half a dozen more of the same glittering trophies in the drawer.

But that was not the only thing in that drawer. In one inconspicuous corner, partially obscured by the obnoxious trophies, rested a small white envelope with a simple gold star stamped on one corner. A small red wax seal rested across the envelope's opening.

Tony lifted the heavy replacement statue onto the table in front of him and slid it into its proper position on his Registration Desk. Turning away from any possible observers, he gently pulled a small rumpled envelope from his inside jacket pocket. On one corner of that envelope was stamped a simple gold star. A red wax seal, torn open exactly one Earth-year earlier, was stuck to the open flap.

Glancing quickly around to make absolutely sure that his indiscretion remained out of view, Tony removed a worn slip of paper from the envelope, and re-read the simply printed message he had first read twelve months before:

> Congratulations! This message is the true and official Grand Prize of the Fifth Intergalactic Toughest Organism Contest. Using your intelligence, strength, bravery, and cunning, you have defeated all other contestants at this Greatest Encounter between sentient warrior species. Following a secret tradition begun after the second such contest, you are both entitled and obligated to return as the Official Registrar of the next tournament, the Sixth Intergalactic Toughest Organism Contest. We look forward to seeing you seated behind the Registration Desk at that future date.

Tony smiled with tender reminiscence as he tucked the cherished slip and its envelope back into his jacket pocket, and then straightening up he brushed a speck of dust from his registration desk. He fiddled briefly with the info screen before he spoke.

"Next," he said.

Rats in the Attic

The early morning sunlight caressed the ornate tile roof of the old mansion as the muted cry of a rousing rooster broke the chill air of yet another dawning day. Of course, the noise was generated electronically, but it sounded real nice and added a distinct country ambiance to the isolated suburban chateau.

Humphrey the butler was awakened with a refreshing 220 volt electric jolt as the rooster's song faded away. As Humphrey was completely electronic himself, this shock was merely invigorating and not at all harmful.

Humphrey was the ultimate in centralized home robotics for the year 2095. Unfortunately, since the year was 2242, this made him pretty old-fashioned and a real fuddy-duddy as an electronic butler. And unlike his more contemporary mobile robotic servants, Humphrey's immense being was physically incorporated into the walls and floors of the mansion. Even his electronic brain was encased in a tarnished sheet metal shell up in the comfy recesses of the attic of the old house, where it had lain undisturbed for 145 years.

As time went on and Humphrey's circuits deteriorated, the various owners of the house found him making a few minor errors in judgment. To remedy this, without tearing out the huge chunks of attic which housed Humphrey's brain, an accessory electronic butler named Nigel was plugged in to assist the occasional bumble to which Humphrey was prone. Of course, Humphrey remained jealously in charge. There was little love lost between the two electro-servo-mechanical servants.

Thoughtfully, Humphrey closed a slightly rusted switch and sent a brisk 280 volt shock to stimulate Nigel's arousal circuits.

"Aargh! Blast! Keep the bloody voltage down, would ya?" Nigel preferred the gentler 220 voltage, as higher currents tended to blow out his more sensitive specialty circuits. As it was, an unfortunate power surge (inadvertently caused by Humphrey the previous winter) had blown out the main circuitry for all of Nigel's exterior viewing phototubes.

"So sorry. A minor miscalculation." Humphrey was the quintessential English butler. He always spoke an octave lower, and a tone quieter, no doubt assisted in this admirable and proper pursuit by a long forgotten blown fuse in his tertiary audio amplifier. "Let's forgive and forget, shall we?"

Nigel harrumphed in an electronic sort of way and ran the morning security program. The outside gates remained magnetically locked, with the twelve-foot-high peripheral security fence unbreached. No human could get in or out, as intended by design. This was, after all, a rather fancy and enormously expensive country mansion.

Nigel's security review showed that the front, back and servant doors were still bolted shut, and bulletproof first- and second-floor windows were undamaged. The estate remained secure.

Humphrey sent a short electric signal to the Man's master bedroom closet to lay out a proper summer day's wardrobe for the current Master of the house, a Mr. Robert Blueberg. A similar signal was sent to Mrs. Fern Blueberg's master dresser, but this unfortunately did not arrive, as a forgotten break in a critical wire had stopped such activities months ago. Since the Bluebergs were not presently in the mansion, it probably did not matter much. And due to the deterioration with time of a few essential transducers, both Humphrey and Nigel remained blissfully unaware of the absence of the humans. It seemed that things were a tad amiss in the Blueberg household.

Nigel remained a bit miffed at his electronic associate. "I can't see a bloomin' thing outside, since you blew out me bloody eyes." He was referring to the afore-mentioned external photoreceptor accident in a rather colloquial manner, but improved his diction after his higher-level quintessential butler circuitries finished warming up.

Humphrey remained cool in the face of the accusation. Well, maybe not that cool, as there was a slight problem with the automatic chiller which was supposed to keep his attic-located brain from overheating. Still, he maintained his aplomb.

"I placed an order for a new visual perception circuit for you with the Master of the House three months ago. Now, we shall get on with the morning's duties, yes?"

The two servants began generating electronic signals to initiate the various appropriate morning motor functions of the house, such as opening doors and curtains, awakening the simple-minded dusting robots, and warming the master bathroom floor. Nigel paused in his standard morning routine and listened with one of his better acoustic receptors. He sent a mild electric tap to Humphrey's non-physical shoulder.

"What's that noise?"

"Hum? Noise?" Humphrey really did not perceive audio signals that well.

"Yes, that atypical low-amplitude irregularly irregular scraping sound. I do believe it correlates with a movement signal, such as that given by pigeons attempting illicit nesting, or perhaps by small to medium rodents accosting delicate machinery, that sort of thing."

Humphrey let electrons whirl through his metal synapses for a moment. "Rodents accosting machinery?" he mused.

"Yes, man, like that. The sounds appear to localize up in the attic. Near where your brain resides." Nigel sounded not a bit concerned, almost as though he were momentarily pleased by this possible threat to his co-servant.

"Near my brain? Oh, my!" Now Humphrey was indeed perturbed. After all, rodents chewing through his wires and circuits would clearly put him out of commission. This potential threat would have to be quickly eliminated.

"We must quickly eliminate this potential threat," Humphrey said. "One must not have rats in one's attic. They may harm the circuitry."

"No doubt," agreed Nigel. "And we do know how difficult it is to work with damaged circuitry, don't we?"

"Humph." Humphrey ignored the rather biting retort. He organized a proper cogitation program to orient himself on the problem.

"Nigel, you must generate a high-frequency audio wave with biphasic tonal modulations," Humphrey ordered. "Such sounds are known to frighten small mammalian creatures into flight." He was somewhat proud of his built-in encyclopedic memory chip. Some days it seemed that only that one piece of his immense system worked according to the original specifications.

"Very good, man." Nigel sounded just a bit too contrite. "Unfortunate that you blew out the necessary audio amplifiers last Christmas, while arranging the New Mormon Tabernacle Choir's rendition of…"

"Well, yes, that could be a handicap. So sorry. Must puzzle this out again." Humphrey might be old, but he could be persistent. "Let's see. We have mammalian organisms. Cellular constraints. Protoplasmic biochemistry. Aha! Poison would be an appropriate remedy, don't you agree?"

Nigel assimilated this idea and electronically nodded his head. "Not bad, old man. Use a tad of the Misses' more potent medications, mixed with a bit of enticing refuse from the garbage disposal, and use a cleaner robot to bring the concoction up and into the attic. Very neat." Nigel continued to cogitate on this possibility. After all, he did not want any real harm to come to his aging associate.

"Say, good man," Nigel continued. "Just where did you store the Misses' drugs?"

"Why, in the accessory store room, under lock and key, of course."

"I see," Nigel said purely figuratively, as his photoreceptors were indeed defunct. "And where did you store the key for the lock, dear associate?"

"The key? Let's see…" Humphrey sent electric pulses in search of the answer to this critical question, but unfortunately, the memory block where such information had been kept was just a touch rusted and no longer fully functional.

"I…don't quite recall," muttered Humphrey in a low-voltage sort of way.

"No matter. The drugs would probably not harm the critters to any extent, anyhow," Nigel reassured his companion. He continued to think through the dilemma. Every now and then, his auditory receptors would pick up more faint scurrying sounds from the attic. He fancied that he might indeed be picking up the sounds of something gnawing through old sheet metal.

"We might send a robo-vac or two up to the attic, to suction up the offensive creatures, and dispose of them," Nigel suggested helpfully.

Humphrey compared this idea with information stored in his still functional encyclopedia. The results were not good.

"Grand idea, young chap, but alas, the robo-vac's most rapid forward velocity is dismally inadequate compared with the average scurrying rate of the currently hypothesized rodent form."

Nigel interpreted this obtuse statement and responded. "Rats too fast, eh?

"Right." Humphrey began to feel a bit frightened. This was the very first time he had ever had to consider his own potential incapacitation or even death as an intellectual entity. His mainline CPU circuits in the attic began to heat up.

A vigilant attic thermostatic mechanism picked up the increased heat production and sent a panicky signal directly to Nigel, as even with that small instrument's limited brain capacity, it had never fully trusted Humphrey. Nigel duly noted the message.

"Your circuits appear to be heating up a bit," Nigel cautioned his associate. "Best to turn down some of your accessory voltage. This does bring to mind that nasty flood you inadvertently caused last year, when you attempted brewing eighteen vats of tea on that one 15 ampere line. There was that one unmonitored relay which heated up something frightful, and then that silly attic thermostat activated the fire sprinkler system. You must recall the atrocious watery deluge which followed, yes?"

Humphrey brightened, and not just figuratively. "That's it!" he cried. "Drown the bloody beasties!" When excited, he too could spout forth bawdy English profanity. Concentration and assistance from Nigel helped him generate even more wattage in the attic, and the worried thermostat signaled Nigel in an even greater state of anxiety.

"Is it working?" Humphrey tried mightily not to appear overly concerned, remembering to be properly British and all that.

Nigel's incoming signals indicated that the irate thermostatic fire suppression circuitry had finally triggered the antique water sprinkler system. He concentrated on the attic sounds with his highly tuned acoustic detectors.

"Yes." Nigel paused to listen again. "I do distinctly hear the sound of valves creaking. And yes," he continued, pleased. "The trickling of water is very apparent now. The fire suppression system does, indeed, appear to have been activated. Jolly good job, eh?" Nigel did not want to mention the additional sounds he was receiving which distinctly implicated electrical shorts. After all, Humphrey had been through enough stress for the time being.

"Ah, good. A job well done." Humphrey felt great waves of relief in a very electronically pleasing fashion. "Do you still perceive those nasty scurrying sounds, Nigel?"

Nigel listened attentively. Aside from a few zips and zaps of shorting electronics, and the closing of valves as the attic temperature cooled and the water sprinkler was deactivated, he could pick up no more of those dangerous noises.

"All clear, now, old buddy. I'll just send a cleaner robot up to the attic to tend to the mess, I will." And Nigel did just that.

After the cleaning robots were through, the offensive remains of the rodent problem were unceremoniously dumped out the garbage shoot, and the butlers were free to concentrate on their next important duty—preparing the midday meal. Unfortunate that their olfactory receptors were long since burned out, as the stench of previously uneaten and decaying food would most certainly have given even the most obstinate robot a momentary pause.

Meanwhile, just outside the house, down in the overgrown garden, and not too far from one of Nigel's burned out photoreceptors, sat two derelict humans, their clothes in tatters. A bundle of recently disposed metallic garbage lay before the smaller middle-aged figure.

"Nothing works!" she cried. "Nothing ever works!" She kicked the clump of junk over to her partner. Her companion, a male, stoically poked at the refuse before him with a stick.

"Seemed like such a champion idea, love," he stated diplomatically. "These automated gardening rodents really should have deactivated those confounded butlers. Can't figure why it didn't work. Just don't understand it." The male seemed more bemused than annoyed.

The woman continued. "I positively cannot fathom another pigeon for supper!" she whimpered. "I simply was not reared to forage in the soil for scraps to eat! What would Mumsy have said?" She sighed, wiping a strand of oily hair from her grimy face. "We really should have replaced those pesky robots."

The man regretfully tossed aside the shorted-out gardening robots and put a not-so-clean arm around his none-too-tidy wife. "Don't worry, Fernsy," he counseled the woman. "Those blasted butlers will some day err. We'll get in. After all, it IS our house."

Mr. and Mrs. Blueberg huddled together dejectedly against the wall. A chunky squirrel twittered loudly on a nearby tree limb, attracting the marooned couple's sudden interest, and they glanced meaningfully at one another.

"Lunch?" Mr. Blueberg offered.

Zombie Heart

"I have some bad news, Mr. Vingman," Dr. Melnick said. "You have had a fairly severe myocardial infarction," the doctor continued to the distressed oldster. Dr. Stanley Melnick was an experienced physician, and had been through this tragic routine countless times. Gently edging closer to the pale patient in the hospital bed, the healer picked absently at an offensive hangnail on his right pinkie.

"I've got some more bad news for you, I'm afraid," he continued, trying not to be overly melodramatic. "Because of your heart attack, a large part of your heart muscle has died. This means that the remaining part of your heart that is still alive is going to be working overtime just to keep your blood flowing normally. From now on, your lungs will always be filling with fluid backed up from your damaged heart, and we'll need to start you on some serious medications to force your heart to continue pumping strongly, and to get rid of that excess fluid."

"Can I have...my own doctor...come and...see me?"

Dr. Stanley Melnick bit gently on his pinkie, trying to get the dead skin tag off with the least amount of pain. "Sure. No problem. What's his name?"

"Doctor...Mangkukulam."

Dr. Melnick scratched an imaginary itch on his well-groomed scalp. "Hum. Doesn't ring a bell. Not on staff here, I take it?"

"No...but he's a...wonderful...doctor..."

"Yes, that's nice, but without hospital privileges here, he cannot practice medicine in this facility. Of course, he can still come to visit you—as a friend."

"He...he can't be my...doctor?" The patient breathed weakly beneath the thin white hospital sheet. The oxygen tubing in his nose fogged slightly as he exhaled. "Can you...call him?"

Dr. Melnick sighed. "Sure. You have the number?"

"It's...86...3...63...0...2." He paused to catch his breath. "Local...number."

"Okay, I'll get to it in just a few minutes." Dr. Melnick scribbled a few more notes into the sick man's chart, and then ambled across the Intensive Care Unit to the nursing station. Flopping down in a vacant chair, he stretched out his legs and picked up the phone.

"Outside line, please," the doctor grumbled into the handset, to the hospital operator. Then he quickly keyed in the private physician's phone number.

"Hello, this is Dr. Melnick. I'd like to speak to Doctor...Hello? You are Mister, uh, Vingman's, uh, physician?" Stan was momentarily surprised to have this man's doctor answer his own phone, without a message service.

"Yes? Well, a few hours ago Mr. Vingman apparently had a rather large anterior myocardial infarction with extension into...I said 'infarction'...'i'—'n'—'f'—'a'—'r'—'c'...This is Mr. Vingman's regular physician, isn't it?...You are?...What is your medical specialty, sir?...'Alternative medicine,' huh?...I see...Well, Mr. Vingman just had a really big heart attack and he wants you to come to visit him...Yes...South City Memorial Hospital...the ICU...no, actually that means 'Intensive Care Unit'...Thank you, too, sir." And Dr. Melnick hung up the phone in poorly concealed disgust.

"Alternative medicine," he stated to no one in particular. "Jeesh."

And with the arrival of the sick man's private doctor a few hours later, he repeated to himself, "Jeesh," because Dr. Mangkukulam was anything but a standard-looking medical professional. Sure, he wore a stylish business suit. Yes, he had on a blasé tie with a little gold tie clip. But the elderly doctor sported a bright red feather poking abruptly out of his tangled grey hair, and with the sun-bleached bone earrings in his elongated earlobes, his image suggested rather pointedly that this old man had never filtered through the standard halls of institutionalized medical training. He completed his ensemble with a tattered old black overcoat hung gracelessly over one arm.

"Aha! My patient! Mr. Vingman!" The strange character tottered into Mr. Vingman's section of the ICU as a white fluff of chicken feather floated off one shoulder. He absently patted the patient's arm as he fingered the standard IV tubing in apparent puzzlement. Mr. Vingman smiled up at this embodiment of medical quackery and quavered, "Help me…will you?"

Dr. Mangkukulam abandoned his examination of the plastic IV tubing and from beneath his overcoat lifted a small, dark leather box. Maneuvering this box in a wide circle over the man's hospital bed, he began humming a discordant little tune.

Dr. Stanley Melnick interrupted in haste. "Please, now, you know the hospital rules. I think. Please, no practicing your, uh, medicine, here. You can talk, just…no funny herbs and things, okay?" Stanley was not consciously jealous of this doctor's relationship with his patient, but he felt very concerned about his patient's continued, albeit guarded, well-being with whatever this weird doctor was planning.

"Oh, so sorry. No use my medicine?" Dr. Mangkukulam truly looked quite perplexed.

"No, I'm sorry. I really am. But we are watching Mr. Vingman very carefully, and we don't want any nonstandard, uh, treatments to intervene—you do understand?" Dr. Melnick was always prepared to bend over backwards to support his patient's personal codes and religious beliefs, but a line had to be drawn when the alleged practice—or malpractice—of medicine was involved.

"Oh, so sorry. Please, then, you must do this." Dr. Mangkukulam handed the strange box over to Dr. Melnick. "Take. And open." He pressed the box into Stanley's unwilling hands. "Open!" Dr. Mangkukulam smiled encouragingly and nodded, revealing a cheerful bunch of misaligned front teeth.

"Ooohhh…" Dr. Melnick suspiciously accepted the dark box and, with a shrug of resignation, pulled off the fibrous strings holding the top tightly on. He flopped the lid off and stared skeptically at the contents.

"Hmmm…" Stanley gingerly poked a well-manicured finger into

the box and stirred the objects within around. There were some colorful pebbles, and a few large beads, and...oh, a freshly amputated chicken foot, and...yuck, a dirty and rotting snake skin, and...gross, something wet and slimy, and...

"Allow me, please, to assist." Dr. Mangkukulam moved closer, poking around with one skinny nicotine-stained finger, and carefully selected a few special items. Then he prudently took back the box and closed its lid. Smiling shyly up at Dr. Melnick, he quickly lowered the box to the floor and then gently placed several wet and sticky items into Stanley's unsure hands, still frozen open in subdued shock after cradling the mysterious box.

The unorthodox old doctor shifted his weight slightly and quietly spoke again. "Now you must say something very, very special. Please, think of it as religious request, yes?"

Sighing, Stanley Melnick accepted his assignment with some regrets. But what the heck, if Mr. Vingman would feel better after this alternative medicine ceremony thing, then fine. Just get the silly thing done with, so he could get on to his next patient. Stan touched his sore pinkie finger, picking resignedly at the dead skin of the hangnail.

"Yes, well?" I'll just repeat whatever words and get going, Stanley thought, not for the first time regretting his rather hasty decision to stick so strictly to hospital regulations.

"Please, hold the chicken foot like so and the frog heart like so. There." The foreign doctor rearranged the animal parts in Dr. Melnick's fumbling hands to his satisfaction. Then he gently turned and guided the nervous doctor closer to Mr. Vingman, who weakly smiled and closed his pale eyelids expectantly.

Dr. Mangkukulam clamped his own eyes tightly shut. Raising his hands, which incidentally had one-inch-long broken nails sprouting from each of the discolored, arthritic fingers, he began to chant. Pausing and squinting at Dr. Melnick, he spoke.

"Please, repeat?"

"Uh, sure." Stanley later could not remember exactly what it was they chanted together, or just how long it took, but he remembered how strange the words sounded and how tongue-tied he felt mouthing them. Finally, after what felt like hours but could not have been much longer than ten or fifteen minutes, the deed appeared to be done, and Dr. Mangkukulam stopped his chanting and lowered his hovering hands.

"Now, good doctor," the strange man began, "will you please strike your palms together, three times, with a steady beat. This is most important. And please," he continued imploringly, "use this pace." And he tapped out a one-beat-per-second tempo with one long fingernail on the bed's metal side rail.

"Yeah. Right away." Stanley clapped his hands together as ordered, feeling the squishy things in his hand splatter disgustingly and then drop to the floor. He self-consciously nudged the bloody items farther under the bed with the toe of his black patent leather shoe. After shifting his gaze down to surreptitiously check for any untoward stain on his starched white doctor's coat, Dr. Melnick sheepish glanced up, and froze in surprise.

Mr. Vingman was sitting up in bed, pink and cheerful, and stretching mightily towards the ceiling. He spoke.

"My, but that is better! Thank you, Dr. Mangkukulam! And thank you too, Dr. Melnick!" Mr. Vingman yawned as he glanced around the room, detaching and tossing aside his oxygen tubing.

"Where's the TV? Yes! Ah, and here's the remote! Say, you guys got any good adult cable stations on this thing?" Mr. Vingman winked suggestively at Stan as he fluffed up his own pillow, and then settled back into his hospital bed, thumbing the TV remote and looking positively comfortable and certifiably healthy.

"Come, we must go!" Dr. Mangkukulam urged Stan. "Can't you see that our patient needs his rest?" And picking up his black leather box and tattered overcoat, he trotted quickly out of the room.

Dr. Melnick shook his head in stunned disbelief and turned to follow the voodoo doctor out the door. He had to catch up to the old fool and ask him a few things, indeed. Despite the assumed medical impossibility, that aged quack had somehow contrived to get the dead part of his patient's heart to start beating again. This event was so unbelievably irregular....

Just then, Stanley noticed something truly bizarre about his little finger that he had not noted previously. At first it felt harmless, but as it continued, it became an irritation. It was associated with that darn hangnail, and seemed to become more blatant as the seconds passed by.

That dead hangnail, on his right pinkie, had begun moving on its own, with a regular and ominous once-a-second twitch. The entire finger seemed to be caught up with the rhythm, and the darn thing simply would not stop beating.

The Alien with the Cookie-Crumb Face

I was watching mean Mrs. Murtle, our crabby live-in housekeeper, move the fresh-baked cookies from the cookie rack to the cookie bowl, when there was a soft knock on the back door. Mrs. Murtle was busy, so I walked over to the back door and opened it. It was Matthew.

"Hi, Lori," he said.

"Hi, Matthew."

Matthew was standing there, outside the door, and he looked carefully around inside the kitchen before he talked to me again.

"Where are your parents, Lori?"

"They're on vacation someplace. I got Mrs. Murtle again." I'd tell him where they went to, but I couldn't pronounce it.

Matthew whispered, "Can you keep a secret?"

I nodded my head. I am five years old, and I don't tell nobody nothing.

"Okay," Matthew said. "I've captured an Alien."

"An elly-man?" I didn't know what he meant.

"No, stupid! An ALIEN. You know, a man from Outer Space. Like a Martian."

"Oooh! Can I see him?" I'd never seen an Ally-en person before.

Matthew looked at me thoughtfully for a second, then said, "Okay. But you gotta promise NOT to laugh. He's real sensitive. Okay?"

"Okay, I promise." I held my hand up in a Brownie oath, even though I wasn't old enough to be a Brownie yet. I turned to ask Mrs. Murtle if I could go.

"Mrs. Murtle, can I go outside and play with Matthew?"

Old Murtie looked up from her cookie-making and frowned. "Yes, I want you out of my way. Go play in the backyard and don't interrupt me if you hurt yourself," she said strictly.

"Okay, I promise." I stepped outside the kitchen door and carefully closed it so that the flies wouldn't get in. Mrs. Murtle had just baked those cookies for a grown-up meeting tonight, and she would get real mad if I let the flies in.

"Where are we going?" I wasn't allowed outside of the backyard by myself.

Matthew motioned me to shush and waved me over to the bottlebrush bush in the corner of the yard. The wood fence behind the bottlebrush plant had a secret hole in it, just big enough for Matthew to sneak through and into my yard.

We crawled behind the bush and I said, "Oh!"

Because there was the Ally-en, sitting on the dirt behind the bush, playing with Matthew's GameKid.

He was my size, and looked kinda like a person, except that he had milky-color skin and had some funny powdery stuff around his small mouth. He had on some funny-looking clothes, but he wore a tool belt around his middle, just like the one Daddy wears when he goes into the garage to play. The Alley-en looked up from the beeping game and stared with his two big pink eyes into my two wide-open brown ones.

"He looks like he's been eating cookies!" I held back a giggle. The powdery stuff around his mouth did look like cookie crumbs.

"Don't laugh! He's real sensitive!" Matthew shushed me again and told the Ally-en who I was.

"This is Lori. She's my next-door neighbor. She's a girl," Matthew explained.

The Ally-en looked me up and down and then went back to Matthew's game. He looked like a kid, but he sure acted like a grown-up.

I turned to Matthew. "What's his name?"

"Phosgi something. I can't pronounce it. But he talks English, sort of. Guess he learned it from TV broadcasts or radio or something."

"Where is he from?"

"I told you, stupid, Outer Space! Can't you ask me something smart for a change?" Matthew got cranky when he had to repeat himself.

"Oh." I watched the Ally-en play the game for a while. Then I thought of a smart question, something maybe Daddy would ask. "What does he eat?"

"I don't know. Probably what we eat."

"Do you think he likes cookies?" I couldn't help staring at the cookie-crumb stuff on his face.

"I guess. You want to try some?" The look on Matthew's face told me that he would like some cookies, too.

So I tippy-toed back into the kitchen and picked up the big bowl of cookies. Mrs. Murtle had gone into the living room to watch her soap show on TV, so I could borrow a couple of cookies for a while. I'm real strong for a girl, and I carried the full bowl of cookies out and back to Matthew and the Ally-en behind the bottlebrush bush.

I set the bowl down between us and watched. The space man looked at me, looked at the cookies, and then went back to his game.

"I guess he needs an example," Matthew said as he took three cookies and crammed them down his mouth. Crumbs spilled everywhere. Boys sure are messy eaters.

I took one cookie and started to nibble it. The Alley-en from space looked up at us, then carefully picked up one cookie, smelled it, and then took a little teeny bite. He looked surprised, and finally said something.

"Oooow." The space man looked unhappy, then pulled a little shiny metal bottle off his tool belt. He used the bottle to carefully sprinkle some white powdery stuff onto the cookie, and took another bite.

"Yum." The Ally-en quickly finished the cookie, then reached for another. This time he sprinkled the stuff from his metal bottle on it first, before he ate it up. "Yum," he said again.

"Can I try some?" I held out my cookie for the space man to sprinkle.

"No! Don't!!" Matthew pushed my hand away. "You can't eat that stuff. HE likes it, but he told me that the stuff he puts on his food is BAD for us. He called it 'sigh-uh-night' or something."

"Oh." I knew about bad food. Once Daddy had eaten some smelly hotdog and barfed and barfed all night long.

"How long has he been here?" My mom says I am very curious, because I ask a lot of questions.

"I don't know. I think for a couple of days, but he never told me."

"Is he staying with you?"

Matthew helped himself to another handful of cookies. The Alley-en did the same, carefully sprinkling his chemical stuff on each cookie before eating it. "No, I just found him behind the gas station on the corner. He was going through the garbage. I think he likes my GameKid, because he followed me home after I showed it to him."

"He must be very hungry," I said. The space man had eaten up all the cookies, all sprinkled with his special stuff, and he was licking his fingers. He must have liked them, because he kept saying "yum" every time he bit into one of the cookies after putting his special powder stuff on it.

Then I jumped. "He ate up all the cookies!" I got real panicky, because Mrs. Murtle had baked them special for her Bridge Building club meeting tonight, with all her old and cranky friends. Boy oh boy, was I gonna be in big trouble.

"Oh, yeah, watch this!" Matthew had a big smile on his face as he turned to the Alley-en person. "Can you make us some more cookies, Space Man?" he asked.

The Alley-en finished licking his fingers and then pulled out another tool from his belt. It was a long spiky thing, and he pointed it at the empty cookie bowl. It make a noise when he did something to it, and a shiny blue light went from the thingy to the cookie bowl. It filled with cookies, looking just like the ones that were in it before.

"See? He can do anything!" Matthew grabbed a cookie and bit it. "Yuck! This isn't a cookie! It's full of salt!" Matthew turned to the Alley-en. "You used salt in the mix. You should have used sugar!"

"Oh, my, I am in trouble. I am in deep trouble," I said, repeating

what I have heard Mom and Dad say to me when I did something bad.
"Don't worry. He just needs to see some sugar. Then he'll get it right." Matthew dumped the salty cookies onto the ground and pushed the empty bowl into my hands. Then he grabbed my elbow and pulled me out of the bushes. "Get back into your kitchen and bring out some sugar, okay?"

"But Mrs. Murtle…"

"Just do it!"

So I tried to sneak back into the kitchen, carrying the empty cookie bowl, but there was nasty Mrs. Murtle standing by the table.

"You stupid little girl! You stole all my gingerbread snaps!" Old Murtie pointed to the empty bowl in my hands.

"But, Mrs. Murtle, Matthew found an Ally-en man and we gave him some cookies and he ate them all up except for the ones Matthew ate and I only ate one or maybe two but he can make some more and…"

"You little lying tramp! That was probably the worst tall tale I have ever heard, and I thought that I have heard them all! Put down that bowl, and get up to your room! No dinner for you tonight!" Mrs. Murtle could get real mean with me when my mommy and daddy weren't home.

Matthew was at the back door now, and he looked real nervous as he spoke to our old housekeeper. "Really, Misses Murtle, we only ate a couple…."

Mean old Murtie glared down at Matthew and then past him at the Ally-en man, who must have walked up behind Matthew. The space man stared at the cross old lady over Matthew's shoulder. She stared back. Then she laughed long and loud but with a nasty look on her face, all the time pointing at the Ally-en man's face. I think that made him real mad, 'cuz he grumbled something terrible and hid behind Matthew.

"You stupid kids! Just look at the cookie crumbs on that kid's face! I'll bet he ate the whole bowl himself. Now what am I supposed to bring to my Bridge Club meeting tonight? What are my dear friends supposed to eat? Humm?"

"Misses Murtle, my mom just baked a bunch of cookies yesterday," Matthew blurted out. I stared at him, as this was news to me. Matthew gulped and went on. "I'll just run over and fetch them for you. Really, my mom won't mind."

"Well, we'll see about that." Mrs. Murtle threw down her apron and walked angrily out of the kitchen.

Matthew grabbed a sugar bag from the coffee server on the counter and hurried out the back door. "Come on, Lori, we don't have much time."

I followed him out, and watched as the Ally-en man took the sugar and touched it and tasted it. Then the Ally-en did his thing again to the cookie bowl, and it filled with cookies. I think he was still mad at old Mrs. Murtle for laughing at him, 'cuz he kept looking up and staring at the back door to the house. Then he whispered something to Matthew, turned, and walked back behind the bottlebrush bush, taking one new cookie with him. I think that after he went through the hole into Matthew's yard he went home, because I never saw him again.

Matthew handed me the bowl of fresh new cookies and also started to leave. "He says to give this batch of cookies only to that lady," he said to me. "And don't eat any! I think he feels very bad that all the cookies got eaten. He told me not to touch them again," Matthew said sadly. Then he also went behind the bush and crawled into his own yard.

So I went back inside and put the full bowl of cookies onto the kitchen counter and went upstairs to my room. I didn't eat any more cookies, but I kept thinking about the day and how funny the Ally-en person had looked and acted. I hoped he would stop being so mad at old Mrs. Murtle, but I can't say that I blame him.

I lay in my bed and thought about how the space man had not even bothered to sprinkle his special powder on that last cookie he had eaten, the one from the bowl he had made for Mrs. Murtle. I think he must have added his "sigh-oh-night" to the whole last batch, because of what he said as he was walking away, eating that last cookie.

He said, "Yum."

Why Cats Lick Their Paws

"Grampa, why is the sky blue?"

Grandpa David had been relaxing in his big padded armchair by the hearth fire, but he stuck his thickened index finger into the open book on his lap and regarded his young grandson. "Why, because that is the color that the air gives to the sunlight, as the light passes through it."

"Oh." Ryan was sprawled on the throw rug in front of the fireplace, studying Dusty the cat. He wiggled on the floor closer to Dusty, who stretched laboriously and then began industriously licking her back.

"Grampa, where does the wind come from?"

David had just found his abandoned spot on the page, and once again gently shifted his gaze back down to his small beloved tormentor. "It comes from moving masses of air, energized by the heat from the sun, young man." Then, more gently, "Any more questions?"

"Nope." Ryan turned his five-year-old attention back to Dusty the cat. The tabby continued to practice her personal hygienic maneuvers, eventually finding an offensive foot to inspect and then lick clean with her little pink tongue. David re-adjusted his position, again opened the old, leather-bound book, and focused on the page he had been studying.

"Grampa, why do cats lick their paws?"

David sighed, closed the fragile tome, and turned to his offspring's offspring. "Why do cats lick their paws?" he repeated the question. "You mean, you don't know?" There was just a hint of a smile in his voice.

"Yeah." Ryan grinned happily and climbed up onto his grandfather's sturdy lap. "Tell me." Ryan thrust his inquisitive face closer to David, so that he could better study the familiar facial wrinkles and twitchings as the old man talked.

Grandpa David carefully placed his old book onto the oak lamp stand next to his chair, and cleared his throat. He paused to arrange his thoughts. "There are many, many ancient stories about cats and about their strange habits. What I am about to tell you was told to me by my grandfather, and to him by his grandfather before him, and so on, for many, many generations. This is a true story. I want you to remember it, so that when you are old like me, you can tell it in time to your own grandchild."

"Okay, Grampa."

"Good boy. Now then, a long time ago, long before you were born, long before I was born, long before even my grandfather's grandfather was born, there lived a group of people in a very ancient land. This was so very long ago, that these people had different customs, and different laws, and a different science. In fact, they knew how to do things that we have forgotten."

"Like what, Grampa?"

"Like spells, and secret potions, and magic!" David chuckled quietly as he saw Ryan's bright eyes widen. "Now, these ancient people were very different from us, but they did share one love that you and I live with today."

Ryan gaped at his grandpa expectantly, barely keeping the next question from spilling out of his mouth. Grandpa smiled and continued.

"They loved cats. But they didn't merely pamper them. They loved their kitties so much so that they actually worshipped them. They prayed to the cats, and treated them better than we treat our own kings and queens and presidents. These cats were bathed and brushed daily, and were given incredibly delicious things to eat. They even slept in their own palaces, and had their own keepers to make sure that all their important feline needs were met."

"Wow!"

"Yes, indeedy. Now these ancient cats looked very much like our Dusty here, with pointy ears, and a long tail, and soft fur covering their bodies. They were quite similar, except for one very, very important difference." David paused dramatically.

"How were they different, Grampa?" Ryan wanted to know.

"Why, these ancient cats were immortal. That means that they could live forever. Of course, there was a big secret as to why they could do this, and only the greatest of the temple wizards were allowed to share this secret."

"What was the secret, Grampa?"

"Now that's a very good question, Ryan. In fact, that question is so good that people have been asking the very same thing for thousands and thousands of years. Everyone wants to know the secret of immortality."

"Yeah," said Ryan. "What is it? An' I forgot—what is 'im-mor-ilidy'?"

"That's okay, son. 'Immortality' means, 'To live forever.' That means, all the kitties in all the kingdom could not get sick or hurt or die. And they could do this only because they had a very special guest actually living on them."

"Who, Grampa?"

"A very small animal, but one so common and so obvious, that no uninformed human ever suspected their magical abilities. That guest was just a teensy, tiny flea." David gazed down at his grandson's intent face.

"A flea?"

"Yes, little boy, a flea. But not an ordinary, everyday house flea. This type of flea was.... magical." He breathed the last word at his grandson and watched for his reaction.

"So?"

"Yes, well, thousands of these magical fleas lived back then, but each and every one inhabited the body of a single cat."

Ryan's face reflected his puzzlement. "Where did they live on the kitty, Gramps?"

"In the ear, of course. In every single cat, in just one ear, there lived a wise old flea. An insect so knowledgeable, so magically endowed with information, that a single flea could tell what the immediate future held for his own cat. And the cat would listen. That way, all the cats with fleas in their ears would always know which way a settling pyramid block would shift, or in which direction a chariot wheel would roll, or along what alley a hungry jackal would be prowling. The fleas would even tell their cats in advance which bowls of milk were spoiling, and which platters of food had started to go bad. And the cats were able to avoid all accidents and illnesses, and so could live forever."

"That's neat, Gramps."

"Yes, very neat. Actually, too neat. With time, the cats became so arrogant, and so egotistical, that they began to purposefully flaunt their superiority over their human tenders. And that was their downfall."

"What happened, Grampa?"

David shifted his weight and sat back in his padded chair. Ryan used the opportunity to rearrange his small frame on his granddaddy's comfortable lap.

"One day, a really powerful wizard invited all of the important people in the kingdom to a grand feast. These people were seated at one long banquet table, and all kinds of yummy foods were placed upon this fancy table for everyone to eat.

"Well, the people were seated and about to begin their feast, when in strolled the cats. All of the cats. They were temple cats, and could strut around wherever they wanted. And even though each flea was whispering feverishly into its own cat's ear to leave, the cats had become so prideful that they stopped, this one time, from listening to their own magical fleas.

"Jumping on the tables, the cats pounced upon the piles of food, sniffing and nibbling from everybody's plates. They licked the wine out of the people's cups, and even grabbed bits of food right off of the diners' forks."

"Gosh, Grampa, that sounds just like last Christmas at Uncle Ted's house."

"Yes, it does, doesn't it? Well, that enormously powerful wizard, the one who had invited all those important people to the feast, got really, really mad, and cast a super-powerful spell over all the cats, over the entire kingdom, and even over the entire world, to change the cats forever. You see, he knew the secret of their perpetual lives, and he knew the one thing that would fix them and stop their arrogance, for good."

Ryan smiled. "I think I know how he did that, Grampa. He got rid of their fleas, didn't he, Grampa, didn't he?"

"You betcha. He made the biggest spell that anyone had ever seen. He made a spell so gigantic, that the magical blast from it flew around the earth three times and then shot out into space and blasted the craters into the moon. He made a flea-proof spell for the cats that would last one thousand years.

"After the shock wave from this spell had blown out into space, the cats discovered that they had lost their fleas, and with them the prescience that told them the future. And the cats became mortal. They were now able to live only a few years before time and destiny caught up with them and ended their individual lives.

"Of course, this happened many thousands of years ago. After the thousand year spell wore off, the fleas returned, but their cats' descendants had become so spread out over the world, that the fleas settled on whatever cat, dog, or other hairy beast they could find. Most fleas retained a little of their previously formidable knowledge, so that most attentive cats today can survive several near-fatal experiences. Because of that, we say cats have nine lives.

"But it just isn't the same. With the special fleas forever separated from their proper cats, the kitties are no longer immortal. And that is why, to this very day, every cat is in constant search for her own special flea."

"But Grampa, how come cats lick their PAWS?"

David smiled down at his grandson. "Why, Ryan, you don't know?" he teased. "You see, that powerful wizard had made his spell so super strong that the fleas forgot just where on the cat they were supposed to go. Some fleas traveled to the fur on the back of the cat, and some to the tummy hairs, and some sought audience up front, in the chest area. So when you see Dusty licking herself, from her tail to her chest, she is really searching for her special flea, who will tell her the future, and give her back her eternal life."

"So that's why Dusty licks her paws, Grampa? She's looking for her flea?"

"Yup. The very last place any cat searches for her magical flea is under her cushy feet and between her stubby toes. And that is why cats lick their paws."

Ryan smiled up at David. "That was great, Gramps."

"Thanks, Ryan." He affectionately patted the little boy's head. Glancing back to his thick leather volume on the lamp stand, Grandpa David surreptitiously reached over to pick it up.

"Grampa, why do dogs wag their tails?"

David retrieved his empty hand as he pondered the new question momentarily, and then gazed fondly down upon his grandson's inquisitive face. "You mean, you don't know?"

"Nope." Ryan eagerly settled in against his grandfather's tummy to listen.

"Why do dogs wag their tails," the old man repeated the question, thoughtfully. "Tell me, son, what do you know about the theory of gravitation?"

Kai's Magic Marbles

The little boy cautiously rolled out his red agate marble and gingerly placed it next to the green cat's-eye. The glass objects clicked softly together as he retrieved the bag of multi-colored spheres that was his constant companion. Kai spilled the remaining contents of the faded blue leather pouch onto his bed. Methodically, he began re-inventorying the shiny objects.

"Green cat's-eye, blue cat's-eye, green cat's-eye, peanut butter 'n jelly, green cat's-eye, agate, agate, butterfly, green cat's-eye." Kai paused to re-distribute the piles of accumulating marbles farther apart. He didn't want to mix them up just yet, or he'd have to start counting them all over again.

The familiar metallic silver sheen of his favorite shooter caught his eye, and Kai reached over to pluck it up. His intense concentration was broken by his mother's urgent call from the hallway.

"Kai! Kai Wong! It's time to go to Grandpa! Clean up your mess, and let's get going!"

"All right, ma." Kai sighed and reluctantly began replacing the pretty marbles into their leather pouch, one by one.

His mother came up to the bedroom door. "Let's go! Hurry up, young man. You'll have time to do that later. We'll have to rush if we want to get any shopping done."

Kai grabbed the rest of the marbles and shoved them into the pouch. He could bring them with him to Grandpa Lee's apartment in Chinatown. Grandpa always had a neat story to tell him about his own antique marble collection. Often Gramps would present Kai with a special marble, something rare and not seen by anyone for dozens and dozens of years. Old Mr. Lee kept lots of these incredible toys hidden deep within some secret place in his bedroom. Why, Grandpa had lived in the two-room flat downtown for as long as Kai could remember, and he had lots of secret hiding places.

"Mom, can I bring my marbles?" But his mother had busied herself getting her purse and keys, so Kai surreptitiously clutched his bag firmly against his stomach and followed his mother out the door and into their waiting minivan.

During the twenty-minute ride from their home in the suburbs to the downtown area, Kai played with the radio until told to stop, then fiddled with the electric window until told to quit, and basically entertained himself as most any eight-year-old would. Long before they had pulled into the small parking space outside of the Chinatown apartment complex, Kai had dozed off, with the early afternoon's hot sunshine drifting through the car window to stir his slumbering thoughts.

"Come on, Kai, let's go see Gung-gung." Mom frequently used Chinese words whenever she felt physically close to her cultural roots. Kai did not consciously pay attention to this, as his past exposures had made all those words easily familiar to him. While he couldn't speak fluent Chinese, he did understand quite a bit. This was very useful when talking to his grandfather, who often punctuated his English with Cantonese words and phrases.

The walk into the building and ride up the elevator to the seventh floor, where Grandpa's cozy apartment was located, woke Kai up fully as he began tingling with anticipation over his grandfather's expected gifts. Kai hoped for another marble or two from the old man's collection, he just never knew what special type might be presented. Would it be an agate? A ghost marble? Or maybe, even, an agate butterfly?? Kai erupted with joy (and maybe just a little avarice) as he recognized his grandfather's stooped form standing alone in the hallway.

"Gung-gung!" The boy rushed up to hug the aged man. Grandpa Lee tousled his grandson's hair as he greeted his daughter and her offspring.

There were the usual formalities of catching up on minor news items, and a brief discussion of the list of things Kai's mother should bring back from the local shopping mall for her elderly father. Finally, Mrs. Wong left Kai in her father's temporary custody and exited the small two-room apartment to complete her afternoon's shopping.

Kai pulled out his leather marble pouch to show his forbearer. He enthusiastically presented his collection to the older man, needlessly explaining the significance of each.

"An' this is my metal ballie. It's not really metal, Gung-gung, but it's real shiny, just like a ball bearing." Kai handed the tiny silvery ball over to his relative. "Neato, huh?"

Grandpa smiled as he examined the bright glass with bent arthritic fingers. "Very nice. Very nice. Most beautiful!"

Then he sighed at long, deep sigh. "You would not have known this, but I have thought and thought for many months, and now I believe you are ready for some very special marbles. Two of them."

Kai yelped in unharnessed anticipation. He bounced up and down off the worn green couch in the humble living room as his grandfather shuffled into the adjacent bedroom. Kai listened to the subsequent rummaging sounds with increasing excitement. He was about to erupt with impatience when the old man finally stepped back into the living room. Grandpa was carrying something very carefully, using both of his arthritic hands.

"You may look at these. But no touching, not with bare hands. Not ever." Grandpa gingerly revealed a worn, old wooden box. The dark brown surface was scratched and faded, and the metal clasp holding the cracked lid was rusted and loose. Kai peered intently at the box as his grandfather gently lifted its lid. A tiny squeak emanated from the old hinges as the box lid fell open.

The young boy stared in dismay at the vessel's plain interior and at the two ordinary marbles contained within. Why, these were no fancy toys, but two standard marbles, one entirely white, and the other completely black. There were no bright streaks of color, or special markings of any kind on the objects. They weren't even that shiny. Kai swallowed his disappointment as he obediently listened to his grandfather's explanation.

"No, these two marbles do not look very decorative. Their appearance is very plain, and I'm sure you would never trade one of your fancy shmancy marbles for either one of these, would you?"

Kai said nothing. His grandfather continued.

"Do not let their simple appearance prejudice you. No, no, these two marbles are truly very unique. And very, very old. There are no other marbles in the world like these two. They are so special, that they each have their very own ancient Chinese name. Do you want to know their names?"

Kai nodded yes. He still was too disappointed to speak.

Grandfather pointed to the two marbles, first the black one, then the white one, without actually touching them with his bare fingers. He seemed to be moving very cautiously.

"This one is named Yin. And this other one, Yang. Do you recognize either of these names?"

"No, Gung-gung." Kai found himself rekindling some dilute interest.

Grandpa continued, almost talking to himself. "I am getting older. I love my daughter, but she would never understand. And her husband, he knows nothing of the old ways. I know of no other person with whom I can trust these. Some day soon, I will be gone, and my possessions scattered among the wrong people."

Then he gazed directly at his grandson. "I know that you value your toys, and treat them well. I must give these very special marbles to you today. But I need you to promise me two things."

Kai nodded again. This was getting somewhat interesting.

"First, do not ever, ever touch these objects with your bare hands. That is the way their very potent form of magic is spread. You can look all you want, but no touching!"

He waited for Kai to nod his head in affirmation, then Grandpa Lee continued. "Second, you must promise me to never separate these two marbles. They must stay close together in their present home, forever. The world will remain safe only with both black and white marble staying put in this little box. You see, the white marble is male, and the black one is female. They complement each other very well. Yang is light, and good. Yin is dark, and evil.

"Now this does not mean that all men are good, and that all women bad—not at all. It is simply an ancient way of classifying this kind of potent magic. The extremes of the colors allow for a blending of their enchantments in life. When placed closely together within this box, their forces are perfectly balanced. When separated, they can cause both unpredictably good occurrences and terrible, horrible trouble. Do you understand me?"

Kai nodded calmly, having been treated to his grandfather's melodramatic behavior frequently in the past. He then asked, "But why keep the dark one, if it's so bad?"

Grandfather Lee frowned. "Too much lightness and good can be as overwhelming as too much evil. When evil is counter-weighted by good, then life is balanced. Now, will you take care of these powerful amulets, and guard them vigilantly, my little grandson?"

"Sure, grandpa. Can I have them now?" Kai took the open wooden box carefully and scrutinized its contents. They sure looked plain, one marble black, and one white, but he obeyed his grandfather and left them untouched and together in their box. He gently closed the lid and gingerly replaced the loose clasp.

Kai then looked up into his grandfather's wrinkled face. "You got any other, uh, PRETTY ones?" He smiled sweetly up at the old man. Sure enough, Grandpa Lee chuckled and moved back into his bedroom. Shortly he returned, handing the little boy one bold blue butterfly marble and two bright red agates.

"Gee, thanks, Gung-gung!"

Kai amused himself with the pretty toys until his mother returned from shopping. He showed her his three new colorful acquisitions, but did not mention the contents of the cracked wooden box. On the way home, however, Kai could not help but wonder about the two secret marbles, and to whom he might be able to show them.

The following day was a school day for Kai. He could scarcely contain himself from sharing his cache until the noon break. Gulping down lunch, he herded his best friend Donnie into a distant corner of the school yard. He showed Donnie his multicolored new marbles, then brought out the ancient cracked box.

"What's in that?" Donnie didn't think something so old could contain anything exciting.

"Just be quiet and look." Kai discreetly popped open the box and allowed his friend to peer at its contents. Donnie shrugged and reached for one of the monocolored spheres.

"Don't! You can't touch them!" Kai motioned his friend away, as he protected Yin and Yang. "The white one's a boy marble, and the black one is a girl," Kai started to explain.

Donnie snickered and grabbed at the old wooden box. The contents bounced out onto the hot asphalt of the playground, and Kai reached out frantically to protect his dangerous treasures. Thinking quickly, he used the wooden box as a scoop to confiscate one marble, without actually touching it, but Donnie grabbed the other one before Kai could reach it.

"I got the girl marble, I got the girl marble!" Donnie chanted maliciously as he danced out of Kai's reach, and turned to run off with the unintended gift. As he started to scamper away, however, his foot caught on a crack on the playground surface and he tripped, landing hard on one arm.

"Ow!" Donnie tried to pick himself up, then noticed his oddly bent forearm. He started to cry.

After the teacher's aid had helped Donnie to the nursing office, Kai patted his backpack to ensure that the old wooden box was still inside. He had safely rescued his black marble from the schoolyard, and now both marbles rested in their aged but secure case. Kai silently vowed that he would never show the two magical spheres to anyone ever again.

Kai was not overly surprised to be summoned to the principal's office later that day. He hunched uncomfortably in the hard oak chair in the outer office as he waited to be let into the inner sanctum. The office secretary smiled at him across her desk.

"Oh, you needn't have such a sorry look, Kai. Mr. Ferguson is very nice, and I'm sure he'll listen to your side of the story." Then, as an afterthought, she added, "You know, he has a son, almost your age. He lives with Mr. Ferguson's ex-wife."

Kai was impressed that such an omnipotent adult person such as the school principal had his own child. "Does he go to school here?" Kai asked, referring to the principal's son, of course.

The secretary lady wrinkled her brow momentarily, as if remembering something unpleasant. Then she smiled at Kai and said, "No, he lives in a different city with his mother. She doesn't let him visit his father very often."

"That's not nice!" blurted Kai.

"Well, hopefully things will change soon. Mr. Ferguson will be meeting with her and her lawyer tomorrow. Maybe after that his son can visit more often."

Brightening, she smiled gently at the little boy. "Don't be afraid of Mr. Ferguson, Kai. He loves children, and he will treat you fairly. Now will you smile for me?"

After what seemed to have been several hours had ticked away on the wall clock, ten minutes later Kai was ultimately ushered into the universally dreaded inner private sanctum of the Principal's Office. He slid guiltily onto the offered chair.

Mr. Ferguson gazed thoughtfully across his neatly cluttered desk at Kai. His brief review of the boy's school records had disclosed that he was a good student and had no history of disciplinary actions. The principal leaned forward in his simple wooden chair to begin his gentle questioning of the child.

"Mr. Wong," he stated slowly and clearly, "please tell me what happened to Donald Kingsley this afternoon during the lunch break." The principal spoke quietly, but with authority.

Kai stared at his twisting hands. He could not seem to find his voice.

Mr. Ferguson tried again to encourage the young boy to share his thoughts. "Kai, it is my job to follow up on any and all accidents on school grounds. You're not necessarily in trouble. Just go ahead and tell me, how did Donnie break his arm?" Mr. Ferguson smiled gently at Kai. There seemed to be a little twinkle in his eye.

Kai tried his best. "Uh…well, you see, I got these marbles, uh, from my Grandpa, and we were playing with them, an' then they spilled out, an' then Donnie slipped…"

Mr. Ferguson wanted to believe the implied accident. "Do you still have the marbles?"

Kai pulled out and opened the old cracked box to discretely show the principal his hazardous possessions. He was mindful not to take them from the open box.

"I see." Mr. Ferguson momentarily glanced at the objects, and then continued. "Donald tripped on the marbles, and broke his arm. All right, then. That's what I figured. Don't worry, he'll miss a little school, but he'll be back in a day or two. Just please, Kai, try not to let this happen again. I would like you to take those toys home, and leave them there."

He smiled gently across at Kai as he stood and opened the door. "I'm sure we won't be discussing any more accidents, young man." And with that final remark, Kai was dismissed from the room.

The secretary in the outer office was again very pleasant. Kai noticed a small placard on her desk that read *Mrs. MacKenzie*. He smiled tentatively back at her.

"You see, it wasn't all that bad, was it?" she asked Kai. She was so nice, and he felt so relieved, that he impulsively took out his secret box.

"Would you like to see some of my marbles?" he asked the kind secretary.

Mrs. MacKenzie looked at the box and smiled engagingly. "Oh, how darling. You know, when I was a little girl, I used to play all kinds of marble games. May I see one?"

Kai felt trapped. Here was this wonderful lady, showing an interest in his new favorite things, yet these toys were dangerous. Well, maybe letting her handle just one marble wouldn't be so bad...

"Okay, here. Take the WHITE one. His name is Yang. He can't hurt you." And Kai made sure that that indicated marble was the only one she touched.

"It's very nice, Kai. And so light!" The secretary lady toyed momentarily with the plain white sphere before handing it back to the boy. He held out the old box, and she dropped the white marble back in. She seemed especially cheerful, radiating happiness and good health. In fact, her face had taken on a slight pinkish flush.

Smiling, the secretary nodded good-bye to the little boy and returned to her work, shuffling papers and preparing to type something up. Kai released his held breath—nothing dramatic had occurred. He slowly walked toward the door marked exit.

Kai, still clutching his magic marble box, was forced to slow his egress as he fiddled ineffectively with the slick doorknob using his one free hand. As he struggled to leave, Kai heard the phone ring. He found himself trying to decide where to set down his magic marble box in order to use both hands to twist the doorknob, when he was startled by Mrs. MacKenzie's suddenly excited voice. Kai jumped a little when the secretary abruptly dropped the phone, stood up, and began gathering her things. At the clatter, Mr. Ferguson came marching out of his office.

"Why Marilyn, what's the matter?" The principal spotted Kai cowering near the doorway, as he patiently waited for his secretary to control her evident agitation.

"I...I was talking with Kai and holding his white marble, and...and someone just called and told me...golly gosh, I'm the new Publisher's Dumpinghouse Sweepstakes Winner! I've just won ten million dollars! I...I don't know what to do! Oh yes, I do...I'm going downtown now, to claim my prize!"

The suddenly wealthy secretary finished gathering her things, and turned toward the door. Seeing Kai still hovering there, she paused and affectionately placed her hand on his shoulder.

"Now Kai, that little white marble has got to be the luckiest charm there is! Don't you dare lose it." Turning to the principal, she added brightly, "Oh, and Mr. Ferguson, I like you, and I love working here, but...I quit. Good-bye!" And she walked briskly out of the office.

Mr. Ferguson stared at the closing outer office door with a bemused look on his kindly face, and then brought his measured gaze down to the Asian boy. Squatting low, he met Kai's stare face to face.

"Hmmm...a lucky marble. Now I'm very happy for Mrs. MacKenzie, but don't you go on in life believing that such a silly thing as 'luck' exists, young man. You must make your own luck. Your marbles weren't so lucky for your friend, uh, Donnie, were they?"

Kai blurted out the whole truth. "No, Mr. Ferguson, but that's 'cuz Donnie grabbed the black one. The black marble is called Yin, and is evil, and causes really, really bad things to happen, but only if you touch it with your bare hand. It's the WHITE marble that is good. That's the one Mrs. MacKenzie picked up, just before the phone rang and told her about the sweepstakes thing."

"Hmm. And where did you find such strange treasures, young man?"

"Gung-gung. My grandpa. He's had them forever, an' gave them to me to take care of." Kai tried not to look scared. "They're supposed to be really, really old. They're magic."

"So...the white marble's the good one, eh?" The principal seemed lost in thought for a moment, then stood up and motioned Kai to follow him back into the inner, private office. The young boy mechanically followed the man in as the door was gently closed behind him and he was encouraged to once again be seated. Mr. Ferguson moved behind his big desk and sat himself down, too. His alert, gentle eyes returned to the boy.

"Now Kai, I don't believe entirely in luck, or in magic amulets, but I do try to recognize opportunity when it knocks...." He seemed to become distracted again, but Kai felt in his young bones that he knew exactly where this conversation was headed.

"You...you want to borrow the marble?" Kai again felt trapped, but was willing to temporarily part with the white marble if Mr. Ferguson would not get him in trouble. He no longer fretted about any consequences, he only wanted to please this personage of highest authority and escape from the current unpleasant situation.

The principal awoke from his contemplations and regarded Kai anew.

"Yes, Mr. Wong, I would really like to borrow a marble, if you will let me. Just the one."

Kai humbly nodded his acquiescence and reached for the old box. Cautiously, he rolled the two secret marbles out onto the desktop. Picking a pencil off the desk, he used it to carefully position the white marble a little closer to the attentive adult.

"Oh, no!" Mr. Ferguson exclaimed, chuckling aloud with the humor of the evident misunderstanding as he pulled on a thick black leather glove and reached for the dark marble. "I don't want the GOOD marble—I want to borrow the BLACK one. I have some business with my ex-wife to attend to. I just need to borrow it for a few days, you understand." There seemed to be a little twinkle in his eye as he gripped the intended object.

It's the Little Things

Old man Astrius brushed the dry bread crumbs from his white linen robe and slowly stood up. He stretched upwards, then belched in a very polite fashion, and patted his full middle. Kicking away the few twigs surrounding the homemade campfire with his sandaled feet, he loosened his rope belt in post-prandial satisfaction.

The two boys reclining in the dry grass opposite him noisily polished off the last specks of food. The boys were not exactly his disciples; Thadeus and Pud were more like two unwilling charges, assigned to the aged magician by their parents for one evening's forced education.

Astrius attempted to break the awkward silence. "How about that barbecue sauce? Never tasted mutton so well cured."

The two boys muttered to themselves. Astrius settled himself back down on the bare earth, and closed his eyes. "Before we view the night sky, I must put out the fire. Observe the magic."

Concentration furrowed the old man's brow. He clenched his fists with a relentless intensity. Beads of sweat appeared like drops of dew upon his brow. Yet the campfire crackled merrily along, ignoring the magician's efforts to control it. The two boys tittered.

Astrius shuddered and relaxed. "Must be the alignment of the stars tonight," he apologized to the kids. "Pud, would you please douse the flames with yonder bucket of sand?"

The older boy did as he was asked, but with the slight lilt in his step suggesting that he had not been deeply shaken by the lapse in magical ability of his evening's tutor.

Astrius tried to explain. "You see," he began, "it is not the great obstacles in life, or the giant forces that we find so difficult to control;

indeed, it's the little things that refuse to bend readily to our wiles."

The two boys whispered something to each other about "little things" and then began giggling uncontrollably.

Astrius stoically ignored them, and allowed his eyes to adjust to the dark prior to initiating his evening's lecture. Tilting his head heavenwards, he began speaking again.

"Look up into the vast panorama of the clear night sky. We find ourselves deep within the woods, far away from our huts, confronted by the dark, deep, blackness of..."

"But, Mr. Asti, sir, we aren't in the woods," the younger of the two boys interrupted.

"Yeah, an' our mums an' dads an' houses are just over yonder hill," added the older boy, with a touch of disgust in his voice.

Astrius sighed again and bowed his head. His short grey beard brushed the front of his tunic as he spoke.

"Thadeus. Pud. Please attend to my thoughts. This place we now find ourselves seated in was once a truly great forest. Years ago, when I was of a younger age, I would lead scores of pure, innocent men-to-be, just like yourselves, to this very spot. Every night we would sit and speak of stars and heavenly things 'til dawn."

Pud cut in again. "Yeah, an' my dad said that if I weren't out of the hut tonight, an' out learnin' stuff from you, he'd clobber me good. Think he's gonna have it with the misses, ya know," Pud added, immediately dispelling any notions regarding his own presumed purity and innocence.

Astrius waited to be sure the interruptions were through, and then resumed his monologue. "As our civilization spreads, the forest is cleared, and yes, we unfortunately do find our journeys taking us hardly beyond our own doorsteps. This does not really matter. What we study is infinite; what we learn is eternal. The brilliant night sky always taunts us, beckoning us onward, tasking our minds to find meaning and our hearts to discover passion."

"Hey, man, that's good," the older boy again burst out. "Maybe had I a stylus and clay, I'd a' note it down."

Little Thadeus wanted to add an observation of his own. "Mr. Asti, sir, what do you mean, 'brilliant night sky'? It's pretty dark up there."

Astrius paused yet again in his lecture. When the silence finally persisted, he restarted his aborted discourse with the requisite explanation.

"Firelight blinds the orbs to the dim coals of the heavens. One must allow one's eyes to acclimate to the dark sky." He poked an arthritic finger first at Pud, then at Thadeus. "Listen well. Stare not at the dead fire, nor at its glowing embers, and you shall indeed be able to visualize greatness beyond anything you have ever imagined."

"Gotta look up, first," giggled the older boy to his younger friend. Astrius tried mightily to disregard the young troglodyte. He cleared his thoughts and found his gaze returning magnetically to the altar of the sky.

"There are myths, and legends, and tales uncountable regarding the grand community of stars made visible only after the sun god has been whisked away upon his royal chariot. Look up, to the north, and you shall fathom the splendor of Ursa Major, the Great Bear."

Astrius felt the warm glow of long familiarity cushion his frail body against the chill evening air. He abruptly brought his gaze down to stare wide-eyed at his young companions. "Ancient legends tell of how this group of stars came to exist when Callisto, the daughter of King Lycaon, became transformed into a bear to hide her from a jealous and angry Juno, and how her young son, Arcas, came hunting one day…"

Thadeus blurted out, "But, Mr. Asti, I can't see none of that. There's a tree branch in my way."

The old magician drew himself up into a more stately seated position. "Fear not," he intoned, "for with my powers, I shall move that offensive branch." And he brought his palms together, tightly, his thin, bare forearms trembling with dynamic tension. Suddenly thrusting his hands upwards, Astrius focused his energies on the impertinent tree branch, and blew strongly towards the bough through pursed lips.

The three stared upwards and surveyed the results of the old man's handiwork. The younger kid was disappointed. "Hey, nothing happened."

Pud leaned over and stage whispered, "Yeah, but I thinks he got the fire embers aglow agin."

Astrius spread his old hands apart beseechingly as he contemplated his two young dispassionate students. "It's the little things," he mourned.

Pud and Thadeus struggled to suppress their snickering. Pud lost his illegitimate battle first and fell backwards, laughter exploding from his convulsing chest. Thadeus, younger and most impressionable, followed his example.

The good magician felt gravely wounded. How was he to instill a universe of knowledge into these children's closed minds when they consistently blockaded their innate curiosities with disruptive joviality? Why, he was not acting as their learned teacher, but as an insipid babysitter! Astrius mentally counted backwards from ten to one in three distinct dead languages before speaking again, reminding himself of the years of exhaustive study and tedious research he had endured to accrue his vast, yet grossly unappreciated, wealth of knowledge.

He seething thoughts pacified, he thought back to the current interruption. The wayward tree branch, oh yes. "Just move over a trifle, Thadeus, and you shall no doubt obtain an excellent viewpoint." Astrius then attempted to retrace his prior thought processes.

"As I was saying, uh, where was I? Oh, yes, the vicinity of the Great Bear. Now, by contemplating the starry fields in this region, we can begin to see the outline of a square box. Form in your minds this mental picture, and note how the outer two bright stars, Merak and Dubhe, point directly towards Polaris, the Pole Star. But perhaps the most catching part of the Great Bear is its tail, made up of the three stars Allioth, Mizar, and Alkaid. Some say this tail is more likely the handle of a giant ladle formed by these same stars. Here we can begin to appreciate the tail of the bear, or handle of the ladle, extending straight out towards Bootes, with its magnificent star Arcturus, 'The Guardian of the Bear.' You can indeed imagine why the Ancients once believed..."

"But Mr. Asti, that bear's tail is straight. Shouldn't it be curvy, like my dog's?"

Pud threw in his two coppers' worth. "Say, you're right, ya are! An' if it were a ladle's handle, now, how could ya carry it, bein' straight an' all? It'd spill. Needs ta have a curve, it does."

Astrius threw up his arms in disgust. "Yes, you two are correct, that tail, the handle, whatever you want to call it, is straight. Always has been. Never seemed to bother anyone before you two, but now I can understand your discomfiture with it, and you are right. Absolutely right." The old man muttered to himself a bit more, and then shrugged in defeat.

"Tell you boys what. You may go back to town. Go play near the village for a bit, and we'll continue this talk at another time. Yes, that's what we'll do. Finish this unfortunate lecture some other night."

He watched sadly as the two youngsters scampered gleefully off into the darkness towards the nearby village. The children of today, he thought to himself, were absolutely impossible to instruct. No respect for their elders, no interest in science and magic, and no affinity for the arts. What was the world coming to?

Astrius sighed in frustration as he forced himself up and compulsively kicked more dirt onto the faintly glowing embers. Things used to be so different, he thought. In the old days, scores of eager young minds would flock to his lectures, attentively absorbing every word and inference. Imagine, complaining about the lack of curvature of Ursa Major's tail!

Glancing up towards that constellation, Astrius hesitated. Squinting his eyes, he stared at the implicated row of stars. By the great Apollo, that starry lineup certainly did look awfully straight! This prominent anomaly was not some small trifle to disregard. Not a little thing at all. Why had he never bothered with it before?

The magician frowned and concentrated intensely upon the double central sun in that imaginary astral tail. Reaching across the intervening eighty-eight light years with his thoughts, Astrius gave the faint celestial object a gentle nudge. He grunted with satisfaction as he watched his selected star distinctly glide ever so slightly out of alignment. Studying his handiwork, the old man noted how the tail of the bear constellation was now unarguably curved.

"That's better," he muttered to no one in particular, and began his solitary hike back up the old trail towards town.

The Living Trust Rubber Company

My shoes were dirty, and they were torn, so I figured it was about time to get a new pair. There comes a time when your toenails start playing peek-a-boo, and when the shoe bottoms get all thinned out and try to flap away on their own. At this point, you really do need to get one of them new pairs of shoes. I did need a new pair, and soon.

I don't fancy those modern-type big department stores, with sales clerks chasing you all over, trying to separate you from your hard-earned cash. I work long hours for my money, when I can find the work, and I'll spend it on what I want when I want it. My sis, she was visiting me last weekend, and she made some comment about my worn old shoes. She even offered me some cash to get a new pair, which pushed kinda hard on my pride button. Taking the hint, I decided that I would go in search of a small, unobnoxious type of a shoe store. One where you could get service without them pushy store clerks.

I knew of one such place. It was on the corner of 5th Street and Wilshire, kinda tucked back up behind a taco stand and at the back of a crumbling parking lot. This shoe store had no blaring lights or fancy signs—it looked like one of them mom and pop places. The name of the store was *O'Shannon's Shoes*, as a hand-painted sign tacked over the door proclaimed in a simple way. The outside of the place reminded me a little of an Irish pub. Besides, it was located right across the street from the car dealer where I had leased my car last month. I remembered spotting this shoe place at that time. It had looked kinda quaint.

So I parked my rental car carefully in the lot, mindful of the potholes, and ambled into this shoe store. There was some Irish-looking guy hammering on the sole of some shoe just behind the counter, so I browsed patiently among the assorted shoes hanging on the walls. Not a great selection, and no name brands, but I was never a man to follow the dictates of fashion. So I poked around for a moment until the hammering dude noticed me.

"Well, now, kin I help yer?" He put down his hammer and got up off his stool, wiping his palms onto his leather apron. Accent sounded Irish, or something, but Mom always taught me that it wasn't polite to question anyone over his or her ancestry, so I got right to the point.

"Hello. I need a new pair of shoes." Kinda obvious, you know, me walking into a shoe store and all.

"Do yer, now?" The man lowered his gaze thoughtfully down towards my feet, and then let out a low whistle. "Now then, old feller, just what kin yer afford?"

I guess I don't look like no millionaire, with those falling-apart old shoes, but I'm not a bum—I pay my bills, and I got my pride. I looked at the guy, looked right into his sparkly green eyes, and answered, "I can afford whatever you got. Just get me a pair of shoes that will last a ways. Something basic, and sturdy, and in a dark color. And maybe with some, you know, scuff-resistant sole, or something." Sounded a little lame, there at the end, but I did want a pair of shoes that would last a bit.

"Sturdy? An' scuff resistant, too, eh?" The clerk seemed to get real concerned over some itch on his scalp before he spoke again.

"Yer know," he continued, with that funny accent, "I got black shoes an' I got brown shoes. I kin hand yer a pair of good, leather shoes that kin last yer six months, maybe a yar."

Then he leaned a little closer, glanced this way and that, before talking again, like he was afraid of someone overhearing him speak. "But I got a new shipment of material, stuff that's new on the market, that has that ol' leather all beat. Made by The Livin' Trust Roobber Company."

He stood up straight again, like he had figured me out and now felt comfortable in letting me in on the secret. Had to admit, he had grabbed me by the interest.

"Okay," I said. Never been much of a conversationalist. Then I added, "Rubber? Is that really better than leather?" Seemed a little unusual, not at all like the black leather work boots I had envisioned purchasing.

"Ooo, yer will like these shoes, yer will," he continued in a merry voice. "Comes from the Oold Country. As fer leather—well, this new-fangled material is a bit like leather, a bit like roobber, but I kin tell yer, it will last yer for yars an' yars." He had that sparkle in his eye again, as he said, "Shur these shoes will last—they're alive!"

Since I wasn't quite sure that I had heard him right, I asked the expected question. "Huh?" I said.

"Well, alive might be one of them poor terms. Shill we say, self-healin'? Yep, self-healin', they er! Scrape their uppers, an' in a day, the scratch is gone. Tear a nubbin out of the sole, and it fixes itself. A lace gets loose, but with a tad of trainin', you kin get it to retie itself, tight."

Yup, sounded kind of crazy, but I was real curious about now, and I needed to see a pair of them self-healing shoes. The idea sounded great. Wonder why no one had ever thought of doing that before? So I said something of the sort to this Irish guy. I said, "Wonder why no one ever thought of doing that before?"

"Ooo, 'twas a secret befar. Secret of the Leprechauns." He twinkled his eyes at me again, before turning and ducking behind some curtain in the back of the shoe store. While waiting for the dude to reappear, I found myself gazing into a dusty mirror on the counter, trying to see if I could get my eyes to twinkle in the same way. It was real difficult. Then the man came back out.

He was cradling a pair of shiny patent-leather looking shoes in his arms, as he continued to speak to me. "The Livin' Trust Roobber Company, it's not truly a roobber product, but an ol' recipe for a coverin' that kin regenerate itself. Has been popular fer yars back where I came from, an' now they have begun sellin' the stuff out har.

Finding a lot of uses for the material, they er," he finished, as he had me sit down on a stool.

"Hmm," he commented, as he gingerly pulled off my old pair of shoes. The tongue of the right shoe fell off, into the bottom, as that shoe was removed. The left shoe had a big crack through the instep, so it was easier for him to pull off. My socks didn't match, but they were clean.

"Yer in need of a new par, alrighty," he stated diplomatically. He slipped the gleaming black shoes onto my feet, the ones from the Living Trust Rubber Company, and added, "Now stand yerself up, there yer are, an' take a gander about. See how yer like 'em."

I did that, and you know, those Living Trust shoes really did feel right. They kind of snuggled tight against my feet, leaving just a touch of room for the toes, and seemed to sigh with delight as I took my first step or two. They were cozy, and warm, and felt just right. I decided I had to get this pair for myself, no matter what the cost.

"Don't yer wear them long the farst dey. One hour, tops. Yer kin let 'em build up thar staminar once they're accustomed ta yer after that."

I nodded in abstract understanding. But the Irish guy, he had more to say. "These har shoes," he added thoughtfully, "should last yer a lifetime. But yer need ta treat this har pair of shoes kinda special. They're a bit like livin' things, they er, an' yer cain't store 'em outside in the cold, or kick 'em under the bed, or mistreat 'em. That would make 'em mean an' spiteful, an' kin cause all kinds o' trouble. Yer got to coddle 'em a bit, an' bond with 'em, afore yer kin truly feel comfy usin' 'em regular."

By then I had paraded back and forth through the little store, and I decided that I loved those shoes. You know, in a dignified masculine sort of way. They snuggled, they responded, and they felt right. I wanted them bad.

So I paid the chunk of money the Irish guy requested. Not really that steep a price for a great pair of shoes that would last a lifetime. As I left, he handed me a printed sheet about their care and feeding (feeding?), but I felt so good walking around, I just stuffed the paper into my pocket as I left.

"Mind yer the potholes!" The dude called out from the open doorway, as I tripped over one. "An' don't yer ferget to bond with 'em!" I heard all that, but I figured the guy was a bit wacko, being from the "Oold Country" and all, so I didn't pay it no mind.

Well, I had one more call to make, by the junkyard, to check for a job. So I drove on over, but there were no offerings today. And getting back in the car, I scuffed my new shoes on a rock.Ced, new shoes and all. So I brushed off the top with the old rag I keep in the glove box, and surprise, they cleaned up real good.

It was late when I got home. I'd been wearing those living shoes all day, just now realizing that the Irish shoe guy had said one hour tops, the first day. Well, they felt fine, maybe a little more scuffed than I'd like for new shoes, but still comfy after more than eight hours of wear.

Although mighty tired, I was cheerful and whistled a bit as I unlocked my apartment door. Walked on in, sat down in my favorite chair, and crossed my right ankle up on my left knee to unlace the shoe.

Darn thing wouldn't untie! Seemed stuck, or something. My foot felt nice, and the shoe fit right, but the knot was stuck on good.

All right, maybe there was a trick or two to this pair of footwear. I tried untying the knot—and broke a nail. I attempted to pry the stuff off with an old shoehorn, but my feet seemed attached for good. Then I remembered the paper that the Irish guy had given me, about taking care of the shoes. I pulled it out of my pocket and started reading, and then reread it again. Some things take two or three ganders before you can digest their meaning, and this paper made my stomach ache.

The sheet said something about congratulations, and about how I now owned the finest et cetera, et cetera. But at the bottom of the paper was a list of *Rules to Follow While Using This Product*.

I don't recall all the rules exactly, but I do recall some of the warnings mentioned in that letter. There was something about one hour max the first day. Oops, too late. And then the paper said something about avoiding prolonged immersion in water so the shoes could "breath," and wiping the uppers off every week with olive oil to "feed" them, and avoiding certain animal fiber doormats and rugs that could cause some kind of allergic reaction.

That was all interesting enough, but what really caught my attention was the bright red print at the bottom of the list, which said, *This is a product of the Living Trust Rubber Company. Be sure to bond with your shoes.*

Bond? Isn't that what glue was for, to hold the sole on?

After the third reading, I began wondering just what I had gotten my sorry life into. How does one "bond" with a shoe? And how do I untie the consarned things?

So I left the things on my feet, lay back in the easy chair, and fell asleep watching the tube. Next thing I knew, it was morning, with my mouth tasting like cat litter and my neck in a bad crink. Getting up to go to the bathroom, I tripped over my feet as one shoelace caught on the chair.

I cursed just a little and kicked my right foot angrily against the floor, banging the heel of the shoe on the linoleum. You know how us men are, when we get angered at immaterial objects. Anyway, with my breath stinking up the air, and my neck still in a vise, I struggled to my feet to answer that urgent call that Mother Nature delighted in waking you up with.

After the toilet and the toothbrush, I sat myself down to a little cereal snack for breakfast, and to decide where I was going to look for handyman work that day. As I cut myself a bagel, I whiffed a bit of an odor. I decided I needed a shower, but realized it would have been kinda hard to get clean when your shoes wouldn't come off.

About then I noticed some tightness and rubbing on the right heel. Yeah, should be expected with new shoes, but as I stood up the dang footwear dug deep into the Achilles part of my right foot, smarting something awful. It was then, as I started to take a step, that I noticed the shoelaces had become entangled. Noticed it all the way to the floor, as my face bounced into the hard linoleum.

Dag nabbit shoes! My neck hurt, my nose was bleeding, and what was left of the cereal was all over the floor. I said a few words I hadn't known I knew as I sat carefully up. I had almost fallen on top of the bagel knife and killed myself, I realized, as I picked up that sharp implement to stick it somewhere out of the way.

Glancing down at my delinquent footwear, I noted that a tight knot in the laces held the shoes together. How in dang blazes had I tied a knot? What kind of practical joke was this?

About then I got this longing for my old stinky shoes, the ones with the loose bottoms, and motivated by frustration, reached down and sliced the new laces open with my bagel knife.

My feet came apart, and inspired by success, I sliced open the laces on both shoes. They fell off with a clunk, and I shoved them into a bag before they could leap back onto my feet or some such nonsense. Believe you me, you'd be fearful too, if you had had this experience of mine.

Well, I felt a bit sad about what I had to do, but nonetheless I bundled them shoes tightly in the bag and drove all the way across town to the mall. You know, the one where the kids like to hang out and gawk at the passers by.

My plan well formulated, I stepped unobtrusively into a big shoe store, the kind where the clerks are too busy to notice you even when they're on a break and you're not. So I slipped the Living Trust Rubber Company shoes out of their baggy prison and placed them down on a shoe rack, next to some fancy things with neon colors and expensive tags. I stuffed the instruction sheet into one shoe, somehow scratching a finger in the act.

Although I felt a tad guilty leaving them there, I figured someone would want to buy those fancy shoes. After all, they were worn just once and still looked kinda new. And somehow the laces I had sliced open had repaired themselves. I was a bit surprised to see this, but then, them shoes were alive, and self-healing, and all.

So I swallowed hard and high-tailed it right outta that store in my mismatched stockinged feet. I trotted back to my car, jumped in and took off for home. Figured I'd just browse through my closet, or maybe the dumpster, and scare up a pair of worn but comfy shoes with no attitude problem.

About a mile or two from my apartment, I heard a loud bang as my rental car did a little swing to one side. A flat! I got out onto the rough asphalt street in my dirty socks and wearily minced back to get out the spare tire in the back. Opening the trunk, I moved aside an old rag and reached down to pull out the new spare. Thank goodness the rental had come with this one new piece of equipment in it.

My hands froze as they brushed against an oddly familiar piece of paper affixed to that tire. It contained a carefully typed message that seemed important, and a list of special details.

But what caught my attention was the bright red print at the bottom of the list.

It said, *This is a product of the Living Trust Rubber Company. Before driving, be sure to bond with your new tire.*

One Sure Cure for Writer's Block

There I sat, glaring at the beige keyboard, unable to type.

I had suffered from this affliction before. There was even a cute name for the condition: "Writer's block." For two years I'd been moderately successful as a columnist for the Tribute, hacking a short piece every week on the computer in the second bedroom we called the study, but it was already Sunday afternoon and I still desperately needed an item for tomorrow morning. My thoughts were scattered, and my fingers couldn't seem to find the right keys.

A creak sounded behind me as the hall doorway was bumped open by Mrs. Blatsky, my wife's weekend cleaning lady. The one comfort my wife accepted was this old Gypsy woman who came every Sunday to help tidy the house. My long-suffering wife, working until midnight every weekend at the campus library, just so we could make ends meet. And the ends were drifting farther apart as I sat there, staring dumbly at the dust-gathering keyboard.

"Tee hee!" Mrs. Blatsky had this comic-book laugh. She'd fire off these short bursts of mirth at the strangest times. We knew her mental dust mop didn't quite touch the cleaning water, but she did do windows. So I ignored her, as usual.

Then I felt a presence hovering behind me. "Whatcha doin', hon?" The question ground into my ears accompanied by a strong garlic fragrance. "Tee hee! Ya don't seem ta be gettin' much typed up now, do ya? Whatsa matter—ya been HEXED?"

So I stretched my arms forwards and cracked my knuckles and turned a bit so the garlic odor wouldn't be fatal.

"No. Nothing much. Just a little writer's block."

"Oh! Tee hee! He's got a hex, he does!" And she shuffled off a few feet to dust the study bookcase.

Suddenly getting an inspiration, I turned back to the recalcitrant keyboard and eagerly arched my fingers over the letters. My little finger depressed the Shift key as I hesitated. The idea was there. It was coming out. There it came. No, not quite. Uh-oh, it's slipping away. My fingers tensed like a field of arthritic thoroughbreds at the starting gate. Now what was that clever thing? It was...uh...nope. It's gone.

A whiff of garlic and a cackle next to my ear made me hop in the chair. I scooted away a bit as I slowly turned to face Mrs. Blatsky.

Her bulbous nose was inches from my face. "Ya need a cure, ya do. An' I got one. Wan' it?"

"Yeah, sure!" I pretended to be eager, but frankly, I just wanted to get that garlic odor away. "What do you suggest?"

"Jus' stay right there! Tee hee!" And she stumbled out of the study. I heard the bang of the hall closet door opening, where the old lady stored her carpet-bag-style purse. What the heck, if she wanted to play witch, I'd play along. What did I have to lose? I felt the computer keys staring accusingly at the back of my head as I stretched again and tried to scare up some idea for a story.

Mrs. Blatsky flew back into the room with her usual disregard of the laws of inertia. Maybe there was a bit of a witch inside her.

"Got it!"

Gosh, I thought to myself, I hope this cure didn't involve eating something stinky. But desperation made me bite my tongue while garlic odor helped me hold my breath. I waited stoically as the old Gypsy lady produced a tiny, old brown leather-bound book. I peered curiously at its archaic hand-written pages as she leafed through them. Seemed kind of dinky for what was being advertised as a witch's cure-all reference.

Old Blatsky noticed my questioning stare. "It's the ABRIDGED version," she tersely explained. Flipping another yellowing page, she seemed to find what she wanted.

Stifling a titter, the old lady muttered a phrase in some Romanian dialect, I suppose, and briskly shut the book. "Okey dokey. I still got them windows ter warsh."

Hmmm. Seemed a mite short for a spell. Well, so much for demonic assistance. I sadly turned back to the stubborn keyboard and got ready to get into a funk. And jumped yet again as these words hissed into my ear from the firing distance of one millimeter.

"But ya gotta be careful! Real careful! Relax, an let them magic fingers of yours dance a jig on that thing ya got there! But, if ya don't wanna break the spell, don't let no accident happen to them fingers! An' 'specially don't ever let 'em touch fire!!"

"Right. Thanks. Really. Much appreciated." I turned back to the computer screen, licked my fingers, and rested my hands on the keys, as Mrs. Blatsky tittered to herself and waggled out of the room.

I sat there in the planned funk for a few minutes, staring off into space, as I searched my blank mind for some idea, any idea, just so I could meet my deadline and get some cheap words out onto the screen. There was some familiar chattering noise from low in front of me, and glancing down, I jumped more than a bit as I saw my fingers dancing on the keyboard, deftly typing lines and phrases despite my clueless brain. I must say, all this jumping was getting me some of that exercise I had promised the wife.

The computer screen was filling up with words, wit, and beautiful phrases describing rainbows and gardens and all kinds of things, stuff I should have been writing if I had been any kind of writer. Page after page appeared on the computer. One article? Heck, I had enough material for three columns, now!

And the words kept pouring out onto the screen. Line after line, it seemed unending. Delicate phrases. Beautiful similes. Fantastic turns of ideas. On and on, for three hours. I heard the front door slam shut, as Mrs. Blatsky left for the day. It was then that I remembered the old bat would not return for another whole week. I felt a stab of anxiety tug at my guts.

My spellbound fingers kept zipping along the keys. Interesting, but I now had enough material for the next few months. I could stop typing. Get those industrious digits to relax. My left hand was starting to experience a distinct cramp, and I became aware of an uncomfortable urge to visit the bathroom.

Type, type, type. Nonstop. Unending. Well, I had asked for it. I silently vowed never, ever again to trust a menially employed Gypsy. A picture popped into my head of my dead skeleton seated at the computer, typing away, the finger bones clicking away at the hard plastic keys, as little brown spiders daintily built cobwebs over the glowing screen.

Inspiration hit as my bladder frantically signaled me that the previously neglected problem was becoming more desperate. What had the old lady said? Something about fire touching my fingers and ruining the spell....

I shoved my feet against the desk, jerking those darn spasmodically twitching fingers away from the keys. Trotting clumsily out of the study, I made my way into the small kitchen, and purposefully bumped the gas stove knob with my hip. The pilot lit the main burner, and I sucked in a deep, fearful breath as I thrust all ten overly articulate wriggling fingers into the hot flame.

I awoke on the floor in a daze, and touched my aching head with burning fingers. I could feel a three-inch gash in my scalp. I groggily recalled a brilliant flash of light, and maybe an explosion, which had thrown me across the kitchen into the dinner table. The kitchen clock chimed 10:00 p.m., and gradually I came to the decision that I'd better get patched up before the wife returned home.

The drive to the local ER allowed me to collect my ragged thoughts. My fingers burned painfully, but at least they had stopped typing against empty air. I lounged in the ER waiting room for my turn while being exposed to a dozen different childhood viruses, thinking over the vast amount of material I had so unwittingly typed up on that computer. Finally, after getting my head stitched and my burned fingers bandaged, I pensively headed home. The fingers hurt bad, but all that twitching and typing action seemed to be gone. And

I had a stockpile of articles to last a while, while my hands healed. With the wife's assistance, those beautiful articles lasted six months, and we actually were accumulating money in the bank. She would print out one composition at a time, and we would mail the work in weeks before the deadline. The six months went by fast as the collection of prepared material slowly dwindled away.

But with the last two magical commentaries sitting on my desk, I was getting worried about the future. Right after our little venture together, Mrs. Blatsky had run off to Romania or somewhere for a prolonged vacation, and now a morbid list of deadlines stared sulkingly from the wall calendar.

Since the accident with the fire, I had not been able to type a single thing. The charmed fingers obstinately refused to repeat their magic.

I called up Dr. Melnick, the ER doc who had fixed up my burns and cut those months ago, and who had become an avid fan of my weekly newspaper articles. I needed advice. He told me to stop by the ER at seven that evening, when his shift was over, and he'd take a look at my hands.

"The second-degree burns have completely healed," he stated as he turned my hands this way and that. "Not even any loss of flexibility or skin adhesions." I exercised the fingers for him, and they seemed to be properly functional.

"I just can't type, Stan," I mournfully explained to him. "I've got a new column due in two weeks, and I haven't written squat for months. Can you help me?"

Dr. Melnick thought a bit, stroking his chin in a very medical manner, and then pulled out his prescription pad. "I've got just the thing for you," he said, scribbling something on the pad, and then he handed over the slip of paper.

Thanking him enthusiastically, I strode cheerfully out of the ER and headed to my car. Not until I had parked and walked into the pharmacy did I glance at the prescription. It was a scribbled note. It said...

I couldn't read it. Someone should teach doctors how to write legibly.

So I showed it to the pharmacist, who handed it back with a puzzled look.

"You mean, you can't read it, either?" I joked lamely with the man. He shrugged. "Sure I can read it. It's just not something that I can help you with."

I didn't know what to say, so I said something.

"Huh?"

The pharmacist poked a well-groomed finger at the slip of paper. "It says, 'Try Dictation.' You figure it out."

Understanding lit my face like a 100 watt bulb in a 1000 watt circuit, so I thanked the man and hurried home. Sure enough, using a tape recorder, I was able to get back to my old style of writing without a hitch. The wife would type it up later, and my writer's block remained a bad memory.

Except that, for some reason, I could never again utter one particular four-letter word, a noun, that started with "f" and ended with "i-r-e." Had to always spell it out. For some reason, my tongue simply refused to say that word.

The Lining behind the Cloud

The man in the dark blue suit adjusted his gold metal frame glasses as he waited for Dr. Stanley Melnick to take his seat at the conference table. An identical administrator in a dark gray suit sat stiffly next to him. Dr. Melnick recognized the gray twin as one of the pencil pushers seen occasionally in the corridors of the hospital. As he had no glasses, gray suit had to content himself with twiddling his gold-plated pen. Other than these two staid administrators and the one nervous doctor, the small conference room was empty.

"Are we ready?" asked the man in blue. Then, to himself, he answered, "Yes."

Smiling at Dr. Melnick, blue man plucked a smooth sheet of paper covered with printed tables off the lacquered table surface in front of him and addressed Stan.

"Hello, Dr. Melnick."

"Uh, hi." Stan didn't know why South City Memorial Hospital administration had asked him to meet with these suits on such short notice, but had been very careful to arrive at the scheduled time. This was less due to courtesy than to the constant underlying fear among all emergency room doctors that they were about to lose their hospital contract. This anxiety is actually quite common among hospital-based physicians, including anesthesiologists, pathologists, and radiologists, as contract termination by hospital administrations was rarely for a specific cause. More often than not, it was on an administrative whim or to get a hot contract for some administrative flunky's ski buddy.

The man in the blue suit continued with a slightly condescending smile. "I'm Kaiser Wilburn, the regional director for fair cost implementation for Balkier Consolidated. We own South City Memorial Hospital, as you are undoubtedly well aware."

"Undoubtedly." Dr. Melnick tried to exude his casual relaxed look by folding his hands together on the table top in front of him. Small sweat streaks from his palms discolored the table surface.

"You do know this gentleman, from your own South City Memorial Hospital Department of Physician Interference, I presume?" He indicated the man in the gray suit. It was more a statement than a question. High-level hospital administrators always assumed that the hospital world revolved around their personal job descriptions.

"Sure, we've passed in the hallway, right?"

"Yeah. In the hallway." Gray boy, lower on the administrative totem pole than the Kaiser dude, had spoken on cue like Pavlov's dog responding to the bell, but without the outward drooling.

Stan tried to surreptitiously wipe a spot of perspiration off the desk top with the sleeve of his white coat. Come on, he thought. Dr. Melnick couldn't help but wonder if he would be leafing through the back of the AMA want ads next month.

"To get to the point," blue man said (Kaiser? What kind of weird sadistic parents would name their son Kaiser?), "we've noticed a rather interesting, uh, trend let us say, in your department."

"Oh." This didn't sound at all good. "In the ER?" Like Stan worked in any other department. Like they thought he was from housekeeping.

"Yes." Blue man paused thoughtfully. He glanced at the sheet of paper in his hand. "The ER."

"The ER," gray guy added reflexively. Somewhere Pavlov struck a hammer and a bell went "ding."

"What, uh, trend are you, uh, referring to?" Dr. Melnick reminded himself to wipe his sweaty palms on his coat before shaking any hands. He hoped he was not appearing obviously disturbed by this news.

Right then, however, he felt that his buttocks could grip a pencil and write a prescription in longhand, he was so tight and shaky.

"To get to the point," the Kaiser guy repeated sanctimoniously, "We at the Central Office have noted a rather interesting tendency among this hospital's ER physicians."

"My ER group?" Stan, if asked, could now tear out the prescription from its pad with his tightening butt muscles. Gluteus maximus right, and gluteus maximus left, fusing as one.

"Yes. It appears that there are several doctors that work in the ER who do not seem to attract the specific clientele that we consider optimal."

Stan was confused. "I'm confused," he stated, wondering exactly what these hospital administrators were trying to insinuate. "You want us to fire one of our doctors? For what?"

Gray suited man now spoke up. "Fire? Oh, no, we couldn't ask you for that!" Although his smile indicated that reprimanding, firing, or shooting a staff physician did occasionally infiltrate his thoughts.

"Right," smiled the blue guy. "Actually, we want to specifically increase a few of your cohorts scheduled hours, that's all." His smile did not quite reach to his metal framed eyes. "You do control the scheduling for your department, do you not?"

Dr. Melnick nodded slowly.

Blue may and gray man simultaneously leaned forward in their seats, like they had been choreographed by a dance instructor form Harvard Business School. Blue suit accusingly waved the page he held, as if it was a moldy union bagel he had picked up at the hospital cafeteria. "Some of your ER doctors tend to attract a statistically larger group of approved managed care patients, while other of your ER doctors seem to treat fewer of the correct demographics."

Gray Suit threw in his two cents in a somewhat smugly self-important way. "The hospital encourages higher numbers of approved insurance clients, Dr. Melnick. Some of your doctors have demonstrated significantly higher admission and acuity rates."

"Oh!" The ER physician nodded. "You mean, you think that some of the guys have 'black clouds'?" A physician with a "black cloud" was known in the ER profession as someone who seemed to magnetically attract large numbers of difficult, complex, and very ill patients during his or her twelve-hour shift. The opposite, a "white cloud," often would bring books and magazines, as nothing ever seemed to happen while they worked. The two administrators smirked as one. They thought Dr. Melnick's terminology was cute. They, of course, answered to a higher level of intimation.

Stan reflected on the old medical superstition about black clouds and white clouds. While these docs often worked similar hours, and similar shifts, the white clouds always seemed to be snoozing in the back room at the start of the next doctor's shift. "Nice night!" Dr. White Cloud would say, stretching and yawning, as they prepared to go home. "Only saw two after midnight." And of course, at that precise moment, as the fresh Dr. Black Cloud stepped into the ER, the paramedic phone would ring shrilly with an incoming run, while simultaneously the hospital operator would cut in on the overhead speaker with the announcement, "Code Blue, sixth floor east. Code Blue, sixth floor east, please," indicating by this cryptic message that some poor soul had just gone into cardiac arrest and the resuscitation team, including the on-duty ER physician, had to rush to that room. Perversely, more and sicker patients meant higher charges and more money for the hospital. Hospital administrators liked that. A lot.

"Yes," Mr. Blue Suit, Kaiser Wilhelm or whatever his name was, agreed, nodding briskly. "Exactly. 'Black clouds.'" He placed the Holy Sheet of Paper down on the altar of the conference room desk and tapped prophetically at it. "We have satisfied ourselves that several members of your ER group have distinct advantages in attracting the appropriate consumer financial mixture. For example, doctors Blithe and Forester do accumulate much higher gross income margins than, say, Dr. Kosmire, for example."

Stan Melnick held his breath. He had always thought of himself as lucky, being a kind of "white cloud," with easy shifts and fewer patients than most of the others. He did not really believe in luck, but his reputation had grown, and the nurses always cheered him in the door when he arrived, knowing that their ensuing shift would most likely be a quiet one. Doctors and nurses seemed a lot less interested in the financial gleanings of their institution than administrators.

Stan shook his head. "But that's all just superstition!" He couldn't believe this conversation was occurring. Maybe he was on some hidden camera show or something. Yet Gray Suit and Blue Suit did not look like TV hosts. Not in the least. And Mr. Blue had indeed made an astute, if not serious, observation. Drs. Blithe and Forester did hold claim to the unofficial but very much recognized black cloud effect.

"But when Blithe is on, all hell breaks loose," Stan Melnick objected. "People seem to come in sicker, and waiting times in the ER are longer. And with Forester, everyone over the age of seventy seems to crump and need immediate intubation and admission to the ICU."

Mr. Blue Kaiser person smiled in a very steely way. "Exactly."

Dr. Melnick frowned. Buttock muscles relaxed considerably, he wiped his moist palms off on his pants. "So what are you asking me to do? I'm not the director of the ER; I just do the monthly schedules for our group." His frown intensified.

Blue and Gray glanced discretely at each other. Gray spoke up.

"We want you to schedule Drs. Blithe and Forester for more shifts."

Stan couldn't frown any more, so he tried raising his eyebrows. The left eyebrow moved upwards quite nicely. No need to visit the gym tomorrow, he was getting a regular workout in this conference room.

"But…but, you see, we, uh, all choose how often and when we want to work. We're a group. All the docs submit their requested hours for the month to me, and I just arrange their shifts, based on what they want. What am I supposed to tell them?"

Mr. Blue nodded. "Just arrange the shifts. Give more to the doctors who admit the more seriously ill patients. You don't need to tell them anything."

"Yeah," added Gray man. "Just look at us. Do you ever hear any announcements when certain nurses are reassigned to other floors?"

Or given pay cuts, or fired, Stan added mentally to himself. Did this mean that these jokers wanted to stack the ER with "black cloud" physicians in order to maximize their hospital profits? Was this legal? Or ethical? Or sane?

"You are not asking me to, uh, fire or terminate, uh, any of our ER doctors, are you?" Stan dreaded having to ask the question, but needed to hear their answer. Would these suits force him to give himself fewer shifts? He was, after all, a "white cloud."

"Oh, heavens, no!" smiled the Kaiser guy. "We could never legally ask you to discharge any one doctor." His smile twitched a bit. "Just decrease the hours. Of those 'white cloud' people. A little at a time."

Dr. Melnick nodded in understanding. He saw where this was going. And in the future, some of those doctors, those 'white clouds,' would maybe find themselves without enough shifts to pay mortgages or send the kids to college. The white clouds would have to leave. And Stan knew that, even though he was being suckered in on this, his turn would eventually come.

"I'm not sure that this is, like, legal," Stan said.

"We understand your feelings completely. We just would like you to know that, on the QT…"

"Don't tell anyone," Mr. Gray interjected.

"…that we would appreciate, in a very financially rewarding way…"

"Very rewarding," Mr. Gray nodded snappily.

"…that your discrete assistance in this matter would be fairly compensated," Kaiser Blue Suit finished.

"Compensated?" Dr. Melnick raised his right eyebrow this time.

"We'll pay cash," put in Mr. Gray Suit. "Increase the shifts for the black clouds, and get rid of the white clouds." He suddenly looked startled, as if he had said something he shouldn't have. Blue suit gave him a momentary disapproving glare, and gray suit cast his eyes down, like a puppy caught peeing on the carpet. If he had had a tail to tuck in, his chair might have shifted with the effort.

Dr. Melnick felt there must be a hidden camera somewhere. In a moment, some TV dude in a loud shirt would jump out from behind a door and congratulate him on his gullibility. Stan let his eyes shift around the room. Where was the camera? In the corner, behind the fake plant? Nope. In the ceiling? Naw, too hard to get the angle of incredulity on his face. Planted on the lapel of Mr. Blue Suit? Stan eyed Blue Boy's fancy lapel pin carefully.

"We'll get back to you on this later," stated the man in the dark blue suit. "But please, you can start adjusting the schedule now." He smiled stiffly. "Got to get those client numbers up, don't we?"

Gray said, "Get those numbers up!" He also stood up, physically demonstrating the concept that both bodies and money were arising. The meeting was over.

Dr. Melnick got up, shook now dry but suddenly clumsy hands with both properly attired administrators, and walked stiffly out the conference room door. The moment for the TV dude to appear had passed, and Stan had the unpleasant sinking feeling in the pit of his stomach that these two suits had been serious. Very serious. And Stan also realized that administration at his hospital would have its way unless somebody rose up to stop them. He had no time to think clearly. Stan had to be back at work that very night.

Stan mulled over his thoughts as he slid into his car and started the engine. He had to return to the hospital in an hour to start his next shift. He thought he knew what he must do in the meantime, however. And he wanted to do it now, before he lost his nerve.

Dr. Melnick drove down the familiar street, the street where he had driven twice a day for the last ten years, on his way back and forth from the ER to his house. To whom could he talk? Who would believe him? How could he prevent this silliness from happening? And was his own job now being threatened?

Stan reached an important conclusion and decided that he knew what he must do next. He steered his car to the side of the street, parking next to the bank of small businesses he had passed by so often over the years. He got out, and entered one particular doorway. He rang a bell and waited.

"I sense that you have come for help," the woman seated behind the counter stated astutely. She reached up and tucked a few black strands of hair under the edge of the flowery scarf she wore tied in a classical way on her head. "Please come into the inner office."

The lady parted sheer curtains and motioned Stan into a darkened room, towards one of two chairs next to an old wooden circular table. On the table were the items of this person's trade. These included what appeared to be a monkey's mummified hand, a glittering crystal ball, and several flickering black candles.

Stan sat down. The gypsy lady sat down opposite him. She inclined her head in a thoughtful, listening pose, watching Dr. Melnick.

"I need a curse, please," Stan said. "On me. And can you do it quickly? I have to be back at work in an hour."

A Taste of Fresh Salmon

It really wasn't my fault. I mean, there was nothin' that I coulda done to remedy the situation. It musta been what they call fate, and now that I'm over the scary part, I ain't bothered by it no more.

The problem started with the wife, that sunny afternoon five or six years ago. The wife was havin' her aunt and uncle over for dinner that night, and wanted to make it a whoop-de-do affair with snacky things and cooked veggies and a big time main dish. The wife, she had a thing for impressin' people, 'specially her uppity relatives.

Wife had been naggin' at me to pick up that main course for hours, and now it was gettin' into afternoon. She'd found me loungin' on the couch, with my favorite red bandana over my face to shut out the bright afternoon glare, not out fetchin' her dinner project. Heck, I was about to go soon anyway.

So she ordered me to go fetch the main course. Not just any chow, mind you, but fish. Yuck! And it had to be salmon. FRESH salmon. "Make sure you get it from SMELLSON'S Market. Not Friedco, but SMELLSON'S. Don't forget! Now GO before they sell out for the day!"

Now I did hate fish, all them bones and all, stickin' in your throat, and I hate eatin' somethin' that never knew how to blink. Yeah, I had one of them phobias, but that's the way I was. Never could eat Chinese, for example, 'cuz of the chicken head included as part of the menu, or them starin' fish eyeballs in the fully fried fish. The fish thing lyin' there on its side, starin' up at me, accusin' me of wantin' to bite it.

Forget it! Just the thought gave me the shakes.

135

So anyway, wifey told me to got get that main course of hers, the FRESH salmon. "And make sure it's FRESH, lazy bones."

"Sure, hon. Like a bloody tooth in a dentist's pliers."

"I'm not joking, mister. I want that fish shiny!"

"Okay, I get it, I'm goin' to the store now," I said, and added under my breath so as she couldn't hear, "Fresh, like a floatin' turd in the toilet bowl." I chuckled a little to myself, as I could be quite a card.

"Make sure the fish you select is bright and shiny! With a fresh ocean odor. And don't forget to check the eyes," she added as I weaned my way out the front door. I was about to ask her what it was about the eyes I was supposed to check for, but afraid of a snappy reaction to my sorry lack of culinary education, I decided to wing it.

So I got myself down the street, sportin' my old hikin' stick, red bandana tied loose-like around my neck. I was walkin' as I always prefer 'cuz I never could figure why a man had to drive three blocks with brakin' and acceleratin' and edgin' into tight parkin' spots and fillin' her up at the pump, when he could just meander down the street, enjoyin' the fresh air and scenery, and incidentally be out of the wife's way for an extra hour or two.

I got to Smellson's Market feelin' all better and relaxed and in a whistlin' mood, up until I stepped up to the fish counter, that is. I was checkin' out them fishes, lookin' for shiny scales and all, sniffin' the ambiance, when I noted there wasn't no salmon. Not like I'd recognize the critter, of course, but I could read the little signs in front of them iced fish. And I knew the wife sure as cobwebs in the corner would know salmon from mackerel in an instant.

"So, uh, any salmon?" I asked hopeful-like to the apron-wearing dude behind the glass iced fish enclosure. "The wife, she sent me here for one fresh salmon. Has to be fresh, ya know," I stated in an effort to hide my lack of fish smarts.

"No, sir, no salmon in the catch today. Sorry. How about a nice side of halibut?"

Oh, shoot. Now I was in big trouble. And I meant BIG trouble, as I knew that wifey meant to have her way with the fresh salmon thing.

"Uh, no, I specifically need salmon. The wife wants, ya know."

The store man shifted his weight from one rubber boot to the other. Now why do them fish mongers in the store wear rubber boots? Never could figure that one out. It's not like they had to wade into the ocean to grab the fishes themselves and needed to keep their socks dry.

"Sorry, no salmon here," fish guy stated casual-like. "Not 'til six a.m. tomorrow morning."

Well, dinner would be that night with the wife's relatives and all, and comin' home empty handed without the slimy object of her desire did not pretty my mental picture of a blissful outcome to this adventure.

"Please, sir, where can I get a nice, big, shiny fresh salmon? I really need it for the wife; she insists. Oh, and she says not from Friedco, either."

The fish man gazed at me for an instant or two, not blinkin' (just like a dead fish, I thought with a chill), and then glanced around like a priest sellin' sex potions. He leaned across the fish stall to whisper somethin' to me.

"Try this little store down the street. They get some real fresh stuff all the time, even when no one else has the stock. Just go two blocks south from here, then one block west, and look for the five-armed starfish in the window. Can't miss it. Just don't say I sent you, okay?" The man's eyes scanned the store again, as if he had just taken an unauthorized siesta. Then he went back to rearrangin' his fish, maybe all fresh, but not a single one named salmon.

So I trotted on over to this pentagram starfish place, nice walk, no complaints there, but with some trepidation that maybe there ain't no salmon to be had this late in the afternoon.

The door was open. I was warm from the walk, so I shuffled right on in. Looked like a regular fish place from the outside, and looked pretty much the same from the inside.

I passed by the long glass ice-filled fish area, and came up to a stained wooden counter barely supportin' the weight of an old iron cash register. Leanin' on the wall behind all this was a man who I deduced was the main proprietor of the establishment.

"Howdy," I began. "Got some fresh salmon?" By now there was just a little tremor in my voice, with my options goin' down and my anxiety goin' up.

The man pointed to the center of the glass stall and blinked. I followed his tip, and saw three or four fishes on their sides, starin' up at me, with a penciled sign in front of them statin', *FRESH SAMON*. No points for spellin', that's true, but I needed the dang fish and didn't care much about written formalities.

I sniffed the air cautiously. "Is this fresh?" I waved in the general direction of the salmon for sale. "The wife specified FRESH, ya know."

The man nodded slowly. "Fresh," he said with a grumblin' accent.

"But they don't look that shiny," I replied, notin' a lot of dull scales despite my lack of expertise. "And just look at those eyes!"

Not that I knew what my reference to the eyes actually meant, but there was a fly or two buzzin' near them salmon, and I had to make my spouse happy or I would bear the consequences.

"Ya, ya, very fresh," this guy said. "You vant fresher, eh?"

"Yes, please. I must have the most recently caught, shiniest possible salmon that was swimmin' around mindin' it's own business in the sea less than an hour ago." There are times under stress where the poetry in my soul spontaneously leaks out.

"Zat so?" The man turned and yelled somethin' foreign into the back part of the small fish shop, a part I hadn't paid any attention to before.

Well, up tottered some elderly grandma with her head covered in a scarf, back bent with age. Would have thought her a fortune teller, 'cept she did have the requisite fish store rubber boots on.

The old lady and Mr. Owner then got into one of them foreign tongue discussions after which granny tittered and wobbled off to the very back of the store. In less than a sparrow's song she was back holdin' a very pretty fish like it was her baby. It musta been the salmon.

I agreed with her in a sign-language way that this fish was the prettiest animal with fins that I had ever encountered. Yeah, it was shiny, and smelled nice, and there was a touch of intelligence or somethin' in the round fish eye that was glarin' up at me. I would have thought I had just encountered this fish swimmin' deep under the ocean waves if I wasn't standin' there on linoleum, breathin' fresh air and all.

The old lady seemed sorry to let the fish go, and kinda reluctantly let the owner guy take it from her. He scolded her, while wrappin' the salmon in clean paper, and tied it, all the while warnin' me to make sure I didn't let it sit out in the sun or get warm, like I was some kind of a fish retard.

I paid the man quite a lot for the thing, but was in no mood to argue as at that moment I needed that fish like I needed air.

As I walked out the door the fish guy called after me to "cook it quick" or some such dire warnin'. I uttered some agreeable thing and quick-stepped myself back down the sidewalk and home to the spouse and her impendin' dinner party.

After the nice stroll back, I grandly entered my home, layin' the catch gently on the kitchen counter like Jason presentin' the golden fleece to one of them Greek queens.

Wifey rustled on over and unwrapped the salmon, pokin' it and lookin' at it real critical like, and pronounced it okay. Not great (that would have given me too many husband points for the day), but just okay.

"You see the eyes," she pointed out. "See?"

"Sure, honey, I picked this one out special just 'cuz of that physical feature. Got it out of a whole selection. This one was the best," I fibbed. Needed them husband points bad.

Fish hunt done, I thought I was done for the evening. Wrong as a rat sniffin' the cheese perched on a coiled spring. Wife had me choppin' vegetables for an hour or so, not that you couldn't eat them whole or nothin', while the fish sat there naked on the counter, sparklin' a bit in a shaft of sunlight. Thought I should mention the "quick cook" order from the foreign fish man, but then I also didn't want wife to start askin' me embarrassin' procurement questions or such.

"Okay," she said as I finished snippin' the turnips. "Now go and gut that fish and scale it so that I can run out and get me a new head of lettuce. The one in the fridge is turning brown on the edges; you'll just have to have that for lunch tomorrow."

Not that I minded old lettuce—I'd eaten that lots of times before, didn't bother me at all—but now she wanted me to physically interact with that unwrapped dead salmon left on the kitchen counter for over an hour. The one she had barely inspected despite my long, forced march to the fish store and back.

Made me feel a tad guilty, leavin' the fish sittin' there in the sunlight when I was told not to let it sit in the sunlight.

But gut the fish? I didn't realize that I had to get personal with this animal. I had figured that the delivery would be the end of my assignments. Didn't plan on becomin' a chef apprentice or nothin'.

Well, wife gave me one of her fiercest unblinkin' stares, meanin' do it or die tryin', 'cuz that end was a certainty if I didn't reach for the scalin' knife, so I sighed quiet-like as I picked up the knife and turned to Mr. Slimy, the bug-eyed salmon. Wanted to run out the door and keep goin', rather than take a knife to this dang fish, but I did as directed as the wife flounced out the door on her emergency visit to the crispy lettuce factory. I heard the car start up and whoosh away.

The salmon was lookin' up at me, hopin' for a reprieve, I imagined, and I touched the very tip of my knife gingerly to its scaly belly. And jerked back a yard as this dead fish jumped.

It flopped again, and then looked like it was tryin' to gulp some air. I wanted to rub my eyes, but the presence of fish oil on my knuckles kept me from doin' that. So I stared back at the thing.

I wished I had clean hands to wipe out my eyes, 'cuz then I noticed that the salmon's mouth was open. Not just open, but full of somethin'. And that somethin' seemed to be climbin' out.

I'd squeezed myself back against the stove, away from that spectacle of resurrection on the counter, and stared at the fish. I must admit that at that moment I was too frightened to angle my way out of the kitchen, much as I wanted to.

There is no tellin' what critters eat out there in the ocean, but I was havin' one of them special encounters of a new kind, as a wet squishy mottled thing eased its way out of that fish mouth. I held my breath as a small blob with two starin' eyes (they had to be eyes, didn't they?) followed by a bunch of tentacles splat out onto the counter, out of the salmon's mouth, while fishy seemed to take another gulp of air and shuddered again.

That zombie octopus freed itself completely and seemed to be observin' its situation, before slowly tentacling its way towards the edge of the counter and in my direction. I noted some small blue circle-like marks on its body, and vaguely recalled somethin' about deadly poisonous blue-ringed octopi killin' beachgoers in Australia.

My attention stayed fixed on that there octopus which looked like it was figurin' out how to get at me when another wiggle of the salmon caught my attention. There was some other sea animal emergin' from the salmon's mouth. This one was another fish, and not necessarily smaller than the salmon, either, but with big sharp teeth and a mean, angry look in its barracuda eyes as it twisted its head in my direction and glared. Strange gurglin' noises and stranger shapes squirmed under the flesh of that salmon, waitin' to spawn.

Now this would be a great beginnin' to a lengthy fish story, but I'll never know, 'cuz at that point the futility of it all just came to me in one of them paradigm shifts, and I grabbed my hikin' stick, whisked that sorry head of lettuce out of the ol' fridge, and I took off out the back door. As I shot out the exit I thought I heard the squeak of the front door as the wife returned from her shoppin' escapade. She always was a fast driver.

Was that a scream followin' me outta the house as I dashed down the back alley? Coulda been, but I wasn't about to become fish food, and I upped my runnin' speed.

After a mile or so, I took a moment to stop for a breath and to tie my bandana around the lettuce head and to the end of my stick. I threw it over my shoulder like I'd seen some hobo do and started walkin' down the street.

I kept on goin', headin' down the road away from the city, ignorin' the whines of sirens I could now hear behind me. Was it a fire? A police chase? Somehow I didn't think so.

I turned a corner down a pretty avenue with wildflowers and trees and kept walkin'.

So that's the path I now stroll, proud as a prince, rich as a pauper, and with no grudges or complaints to speak of. Never did find out what the ol' wife encountered in that kitchen, comin' out of that bewitched salmon, but whatever it was, it was no longer any concern of mine.

I love the free life. I go where I go, do what I do, sleep when I want, and eat what I can scrounge. As long as it ain't fish.

Printed in the United Kingdom
by Lightning Source UK Ltd.
109148UKS00001B/147